DJINN AND BEAR IT

DJINN AND BEAR IT

PROVIDENCE PARANORMAL COLLEGE BOOK FIVE

D.R. PERRY

DISRUPTIVE IMAGINATION

LMBPN Publishing
PMB 196, 2540 South Maryland Pkwy
Las Vegas, NV 89109

Version 2.0 May, 2021
ebook ISBN: 978-1-64971-716-0
Print ISBN: 978-1-64971-717-7

CHAPTER ONE

Jeannie

I'd been hanging around in a park by the water, minding my own business, which sucked. Staying in Newport after finding out my ex-boyfriend Dale cheated on me wouldn't have been possible if a friend hadn't paid for me to have a new room. And then, I'd found out his stepfather died in some kind of freak accident. So there I was, killing time until another friend picked me up for a jaunt by the Newport Police Station and then the funeral. So I sat there mentally preparing myself for the worst day ever. Unlike police interviews, I was used to funerals but hadn't ever been to one for a dragon shifter.

My suitcase and most of my clothes had bullet holes in them. Olivia Adler was bringing me something more appropriate for both occasions than retro pink acid-wash leggings with two suspiciously round rips and the old Night Creatures concert tee I usually slept in. I looked down at the shirt with its fanged design surrounding the letters "NC." Dale had bought me that shirt during better days in our relationship, before I'd gotten the acceptance letter to Providence Paranormal's first open admissions and he didn't. He'd begged me not to leave, said he'd go crazy with me out of town so much. If only I knew at the time that meant he'd go crazy banging other girls until he knocked one up.

I sighed, putting my head in my hands. When Dale's girl on the side showed up in Newport to show me her baby belly in person, that was the end. I glanced out at the ocean, but couldn't bear looking at it and cast my eyes down instead. And that's when I saw the green thing on the other side of the rail. It looked like maybe copper or brass and wedged between some rocks on the shoreline. I leaned over the side to get a better look. Yup, it had to be some kind of metal, pretty badly tarnished, too.

Ducking under the rail was a much better idea than hopping it. I wore my least damaged shoes, white patent pumps with inch and a half heels. Even in flats I'd have had to tread carefully. With these shoes, getting over the rocks to snag whatever lost treasure waited among them was almost like trying to get around in those four-foot snowbanks we'd had over the winter.

"Ow!" My ankle strained as I snagged the handle on the back of the metal thing. I tiptoed back to the rail and under it again, glad I hadn't broken my neck. And finally, I had time to get a good look at my prize.

Well, not really. I held an old lamp, the oil-burning kind. I couldn't be sure, but I thought I'd seen it before when I toured The Academy and then again more recently. Yes, this could be the lamp I'd seen in the basement lounge during the Winter intersession, but it was hard to be sure. Seawater only made green tarnish on certain metals, but was the lamp copper or brass? I figured there was only one way to find out.

I used the hem of my shirt to rub some of the tarnish off, and the lamp instantly warmed in my hands. I almost dropped it. A piece of metal washed up in mid-March should be cold, like it had been when I'd picked it up. And it shouldn't be spewing deep purple smoke from the end the wick's supposed to go in either. I took a deep breath and set it down on the bench next to me instead of dropping the dang thing. Good thing I did, too. The smoke coming from it got so thick that I couldn't see.

Even before the smoke cleared, I felt the presence beside me on the bench and knew I'd be meeting a Djinn. When I could look at the person who'd materialized to my right, the first thing I noticed was that the mostly tarnished lamp squatted between us like the world's weirdest chaperon. I almost giggled at that. I was nearly twenty-five and hardly qualified as the kind of girl who needed supervision. As a Resident Assistant, usually, I was the one doing that job.

"Ismail, at your service." He had a swarthy complexion that made the whiteness of his teeth stand out, and his hair was a smoky black. His dimple-framed smile was almost too bashful and cutesy to be traditionally handsome. "In case you weren't aware, I'm a Djinn, and you have claim to my lamp until I've completed three tasks for you."

"Hi, I'm Jeannie. Jeannie La Montagne." I stuck out my hand, wondering why I'd given him the lame Dorothy-Gale-from-Kansas self-introduction. Lamer than if I'd broken the heel off one of my pumps on the way over the rocks.

"Well, Jeannie Jeannie La Montagne, it is good to meet you." A different kind of man might have sounded like he was mocking me. Not Ismail. His big brown eyes held nothing but formality, so why did I have goosebumps? Could it be him?

"It's good to meet you, too, but I honestly don't think I need a Djinn." I winced a bit even though Ismail didn't seem unhappy to hear that. "I mean, I'm only a college student. We don't have too many life-or-death situations that we have to wish our way out of or anything."

"Coincidence never chooses wrong." Ismail's smile dimmed

down into something more like a gentle grin. "I'm sure you'll think of something."

"Oh." I hadn't heard the crunch of shoes on gravel as Olivia approached. "Was I interrupting? It's just that we're already going to be late for your interrogation, and you still have to change. And then, there's the Air dragon's Mourning Day ceremony."

I sighed and shook my head, feeling like the world's biggest idiot. I'd just gone on about having no life or death problems, and Olivia had walked up and mentioned a dragon funeral. I should have expected as much. The owl shifter was helpful to a fault, but also unflinchingly honest. That was just peachy for her future career in Extrahuman Law but not so amazing for people like me. I wondered whether she'd ever heard of little white lies or even the concept of putting things delicately. Or maybe I was oversensitive because I'd had a rough week.

"Okay." I gazed out at the little parking lot, noticing that Olivia's car was one of those tiny Smart cars. Not the best vehicle for driving around with a woman who turned into a half-ton bear, or for carting extra Djinn passengers. Was Ismail solid when he came out of his lamp or more like a visible ghost? I wondered whether he'd need a seat belt.

"There can only be one air dragon having a Mourning Day in Newport." Ismail blinked gravely at me. "If you think it is appropriate, mistress, I would like to emerge from the lamp to pay my respects to Wilfred Harcourt."

"Um, okay." I winced inwardly at the term he used to address me, but the Djinn wouldn't know I'd been cheated on recently. Besides, his clothes and mannerisms told me he'd been in that lamp for a long time. Maybe "mistress" didn't mean the other woman back in his day. "But I think the car's too small for all three of us."

"I will return to my lamp for the drive, then, if that's acceptable."

"Look, Ismail." I stood up, smoothing out my t-shirt. "I don't want you to think you have to take my orders about something like that. I don't know much about claiming Djinn lamps, but I'm giving you permission to go ahead and decide for yourself when to come and go from your lamp. Also, I'm not a primary school teacher. You don't need a hall pass to use the restroom. And call me Jeannie, please."

"Thank you, Jeannie." He gave me a slight bow. "I will see you once we get to the Mourning Day ceremony."

Olivia and I watched him go back into his lamp. It was like the time in Chem lab when we did an experiment. The indigo beads of iodine in the flask turned into purple smoke, a reaction the professor called sublimation. Ismail did that. He went smoky, except that it was blue smoke instead of iodine's purple hue.

"Hoo, boy." Olivia flipped her hair over one shoulder. "Looks like you got yourself an Unseelie Djinn, Jeannie."

"Yeah, looks like it." I picked up the lamp in one hand and my bullet-scarred suitcase with the other.

"Believe it or not, the Unseelie kind is easier for folks who aren't used to dealing with Faeries." Olivia's trivia-filled chatter was one of the reasons I liked her.

"Really?"

"Yeah." She opened the driver-side door and got in. Olivia's obliviousness when on one of her tangents was one of the reasons not everyone liked her. "Unseelie Fae go by the spirit of the law, not the letter. They can give you a pass if they like you. And I think this one does. Like you, I mean."

I tucked the suitcase behind the seat and got into the car. Ismail's lamp went on the floor between my feet. Olivia drove us down the road to a gas station. When I went to the restroom to change, I left the lamp with my friend. I had no idea whether a Djinn could see me from inside his lamp if I brought it to the bathroom with me, but I didn't want to find out.

Once dressed and back in the car, I put the lamp in my bag and we rode along in silence. Olivia seemed to be on one of the ultra-focus trips her Adderal induced. Supposedly, the owl shifter took that so she could be diurnal. Whatever the reason, I always wondered what she'd be like if she kept to a night schedule like other nocturnally inclined Extrahumans. And then, I wondered why. It wasn't her Extrahuman Law major. PPC ran that one on both day and night schedules.

When we pulled up to the police station, I wiped my clammy palms on the rumpled t-shirt in my bag. Olivia noticed and tilted her head as she focused her eyes on me.

"It can't be that bad, Jeannie." She blinked big amber eyes. "If something were wrong, you'd be meeting Weaver and Klein at night when they're both powerhouses."

"Thanks." I got out of the car, leaving Olivia to wait as I tried to let her words comfort me. They didn't do much. Not that I didn't believe her, but spider shifters were scary. Most vampires, not so much.

The desk Sargent waved me along, gesturing down a hall. Detective Weaver stood there, six-foot-nothing and spindly. I looked up, not sure whether I should smile. I did it anyway and felt like an idiot when she brought me into the basement and then to an honest-to-goodness interrogation room.

Detective Klein ruined the effect by waving at me from the chair. He got up, pulled it out for me, and gestured at the cup of coffee within easy reach. Even though his smile bared his fangs, I could tell Klein was the good cop. I figured I'd better sit, so I did. When I took a sip of the coffee, my eyebrows felt like they'd actually go into my hair.

"We heard you liked mocha, so here it is." I almost gave myself whiplash turning my head to look at Detective Weaver. The dour expression she'd worn the night of the shooting and all the way down into the basement got replaced by a thread-thin smile.

"Wow, thanks." I sipped again, less tentatively this time. "I wasn't sure what to expect, but this wouldn't have been on the list."

"We're the Newport PD, not the Spanish Inquisition." Detective Weaver shrugged. "And don't tell anyone I spouted off a Monty Python line, or I'll take that mocha away." She actually winked. "I want to know why you think you're here."

"You have more questions for me." I blinked, not sure why what I thought about police procedure mattered.

"That's only part of it." Detective Klein half-sat on the table. He still wore the dorky orange puffy vest that looked like something from a cheesy 80s movie. I wondered whether he might actually be from the 80s, especially with his majestic mullet.

"Okay, then." I leaned back, cupping both hands around my coffee cup. My handbag strap caught on the back of the chair, and I almost tipped it over. "Woah!"

In a flash, Detective Weaver was there catching my chair. I knew spider shifters were fast but hadn't actually seen one in action. And then I realized she hadn't caught it with her hands. A handful of gossamer strands led from her fingers to my seat, steadying it.

"Thanks." I let out an exasperated breath. "I don't know what's going on with me today. Is it national bear klutzes day or something?"

Klein unleashed a belly-laugh. I felt like I was on campus with the other students instead of a police station. This wasn't supposed to happen, was it? I must have looked as confused as I felt because Weaver snapped her fingers at the threads, then put the serious back on her face.

"Look, we're mainly bringing you here to tell you things are still dangerous out there." She leaned against the wall by the doorway. "We're almost sure the shooters were part of the Gatto Gang. What we aren't sure about is who was the target. And that's where the questions come in. So, along the lines of why you think you're in here, why do you think a big cat shifter Mafia would want you dead?"

I froze for just a split second, nearly twenty years of guilt stopping me cold. And then it lifted, like it usually did. Too late, though. Both Weaver and Klein had noticed my reaction. I'd have to tell them something. I wracked my brain, knowing they'd think I was really a dumb blonde, despite being one of the first shifters accepted to PPC.

"Well, I was in the Boston Internment. That's pretty common knowledge since I let my classmates interview me about it for projects." I looked at Klein when I spoke, knowing he'd be the one checking the physical signs of lying. Vampires were good at that, of course.

"So you don't think it's got anything to do with the fact that you're friends with the Harcourt kid?" Klein had his hands in the pocket of his goofy vest.

"No. I mean, I'm the Resident Assistant in the dorm at school. It's not like we're bosom buddies."

"We know he paid for you to stay in Newport after the er, altercation with Dale Parker."

"Yeah, but that might be because I lent my room to one of his packmates a few weeks back."

"Huh." Klein pulled a ball-point pen from his pocket, the kind where the tip pops in and out with a button. He pressed it a few times, slowly. "Yeah, that checks out. He's in the Dennison kid's pack. Shifters with Hats or something like that."

"Tinfoil Hat," Weaver corrected. She eyed the pen warily. "So, can you think of anything else besides the Internment?"

"Actually, there is one thing." I shook my head. "I couldn't have been the target at all." I stared into my coffee, unable to block out the sound of Klein's pen clicking.

"And why is that?" Detective Weaver reminded me of Professor Watkins all of a sudden. I wondered whether they might be related.

"That car wasn't parked. It couldn't have been waiting for me." My explanation was peppered with Klein's noisy pen clicking habit. "I heard the engine, and it was active, not in idle. There's no way big cat shifters could have predicted the exact moment I'd be storming out of the bed-and-breakfast. But Blaine and his lady friend were walking to a dinner reservation. That's information someone could have gotten, nice and predictable. The shooter had to be after one of them."

"See, I told you." Weaver strode over to Klein and snatched the pen right out of his hand. "She figured it out. You owe me twenty bucks."

"Who'd have thought, huh?" Klein shook his head and produced a wallet from his back pocket. "On the same night, I met two ladies who could be detectives someday." He handed Weaver a twenty, then put the wallet away.

"Not me, I'm going into Social Services." I grinned. "I use my powers of deduction to help elderly Extrahumans. They can be a dodgy bunch, so there are probably some transferable skills there."

"Well, I look forward to seeing you in a more professional capacity in the future." Weaver smiled her thready smile again and opened the door. "You're free to go. Thanks."

I stumbled on the way out and spilled my mocha coffee all over the floor in front of the desk sergeant. If I didn't get it together, the Gitano Gang might just try to take me out for being a clumsiness menace in their territory.

CHAPTER TWO

Ismail

I paced the room I'd lived in for almost a century. My feet couldn't wear holes in the thick woolen carpets. That came with the power of serving in a lamp. Everything here would stay as I wished, the prison I'd agreed to do time in was utterly mine. And that's as it should be. The Goblin King wasn't the one who had to live in here. And I had more than enough power to bend it to my will.

I'd opted to serve, cut myself off from the world to escape being an Armenian man conscripted into the Turkish army. I could choose to see and hear events outside within a thousand miles. And I could even come out to be present with whoever mastered the lamp and the surrounding people. I spent more time outside the lamp than in, back then. I'd had a family out there.

And now, I believed I had no one of consequence to bother visiting with. Just a woman about the age I'd been when I got out of the Under after my time tithing to the King. I listened to her deliberately idle chatter with the girl who'd come to drive her away, noting how she guided the conversation to make the more awkward owl shifter comfortable.

At the police station, I thought she might make a wish to get out of trouble with the police, but she wasn't in any. Instead, they were concerned for her. Who was this Jeannie La Montagne, to engender such consideration, such camaraderie with Detectives used to second-guessing everyone around them? Dangerous, that's what. I'd have to be careful with someone like her as the lamp's master. She could call on me to use my power in ways I'd have trouble understanding.

In the foyer, when she spilled her coffee, I had almost caught it. But I wondered, why should I? I'd been paralyzed, unable to do anything for my family a century ago, so why rescue this girl? Hot coffee was nothing compared to the atrocities of war, after all. As with the lamp's last master, I acted with subtlety without leaving my safe place. I diverted the liquid, so none of it splashed her funeral attire. I found I had to draw on more power than expected in order to do it, as though something was working against me. But I thought it didn't matter.

The car ride to Wilfred's Mourning Day passed with no conversation over the woman on the radio singing about how when she calls, her former lover never seemed to be home. I stayed in my lamp until we were out on the Harcourt mansion's back lawn, watching my new master drop a ring in the urn and her owl friend leave a feather.

When Kimiko Ichiro brought me there only days before, I'd hoped to see Wilfred again, speak with him, pay him a visit and see the rare egg he and his wife had managed to get. All I had now to pay Wilfred Harcourt, the man who did what I couldn't by saving my children and neighbors, were respects. When I vanished myself out of the lamp in order to pay my token, everyone noticed.

"Ismail, I'm so glad you're not at the bottom of the bay!" The Tanuki girl grabbed my free hand before I could avoid her. I immediately sensed the telepathic link between her and Wilfred's stepson, although I had no idea what they conveyed through it, of course.

"I'd still be waterlogged if it hadn't been for Miss La Montagne." I nodded at my new master and tried my best not to stare. The dark suit became her, a far cry from the ragged clothing she'd worn when we met. I'd need to steel myself if I wanted to avoid falling victim to whatever unconscious charm she exuded, so I focused on the event at hand instead. "I'm sorry about—"

"Don't you dare, Ismail." Kimiko Ichiro let go of my hands and crossed her arms over her chest. "Coincidence sucks. I won't let you think what happened to Wilfred was your fault. Remember, I was the one with the wishes."

I nodded, unable to say anything else. She didn't know about Yeva, our children, or what the man we mourned meant to me. Explanations weren't part of the Djinn contract. I said nothing, just sighed and dropped a ring of my own into the urn. The old air dragon had always coveted it, so now his stepson could have it instead. Its front could open, the inside contained a note I'd written just that afternoon. Once Wilfred's own child hatched, Blaine would find instructions to pass that ring on.

I walked away across the lawn, back toward the tiny car I wouldn't fit in, not sure I wanted to be alone. As I was about to go back into the lamp, Jeannie stopped beside me. I stood next to her. She turned to face me, putting one hand on my arm. It tingled a bit, and I wondered why, especially because shifters didn't have magical energy unless in the process of changing forms.

"Ismail, I'm so sorry." Her big blue eyes held nothing but sincerity. I wasn't sure what to do with that. Most people had ulterior motives around a Djinn.

"Thank you." Giving the correct response to sympathy had become automatic since my wife's death. Wilfred used to trot me out whenever he wanted to tell the story of how he'd rescued Armenians during the Turkish genocide, though he'd done it less frequently after he saved Saul Kazynski from the Nazis decades later. Heroes weren't always the sort of people who did everything right. The Extrahuman kind were even more flawed than the ones non-magical folk wrote and read about in their comic books.

"I was just here because I know Blaine." She patted my arm a few times before taking her hand away. "Did you know he took a metric truck-ton of gunfire to protect Kim and me?"

"Yes. And I bet he complained about his clothes afterward, too." The corners of my mouth turned up. "Unsurprising, considering the example he had growing up."

"How did you know Wilfred, anyway?"

"It's a long story." I hadn't talked about it in my own words, so the fact that I wanted to answer Jeannie's question came as a surprise. A frightening one, at that. I tried not to narrow my eyes as I wondered whether she had Psychics in her family. "This isn't really the time or place for it."

"Some other time, then." She nodded without smiling. I wondered whether her air of sympathy was practiced, then stopped that train of thought. Jeannie La Montagne was too young to have much experience pretending at this sort of thing. She was a bear shifter, not a Sidhe or an immortal dragon, though she was lovely enough to have either in her ancestry.

"As you wish."

I vanished myself back into my lamp, both to cover for my sudden awkwardness and so we'd all fit in the tiny automobile. The last thing I heard was Olivia Adler's hooted exclamation.

"Hoo boy! That's weird."

Like most of her kind, the owl shifter was right in more ways than she'd intended. Serving Jeannie La Montagne just might turn out to be the strangest experience of my long life. It also might not end my servitude in the lamp. I'd scanned as many records as I'd been able to on the sly since Kimiko Ichiro wished herself out of the Academy and found nothing about my family. Without a tithed blood relative or Pure Faerie to take over, I'd be stuck in this lamp forever.

A week ago that might have suited me just fine. I wondered where my new, muddled feelings came from?

CHAPTER THREE

Jeannie

I shrieked as the water in the shower ran cold, unable to figure out why it happened every time I'd showered since I got back from Newport. I'd gotten tired of it after the first week. Here it was, the last week in April, and the cold water kept on going like the Energizer bunny.

No matter what time I tried, or which bathroom I used, I got what felt like six seconds of hot water and then the Ice Bucket Challenge. And to top it all off, I'd seemingly turned into the biggest klutz in the known universe since the end of Spring Break. Bumping, dropping, slipping, and tripping had taken a toll on my clothes and belongings, even if my fast shifter healing meant the bruises faded in minutes.

"Ow!" I slipped and fell, bruising my tailbone on wet tile. Even worse, I'd taken the shower curtain with me. Water ricocheted off it in a fine, cold spray, getting me right in the face. When I reached for the knob to shut the water off, I bumped my head. "I wish I was back in bed."

I flinched away as the bathroom filled with steam, thinking the water had gone scalding. It hadn't. A blue-suited figure stood between the shower and the sink. I stopped struggling to get untangled from the vinyl shower curtain, wrapping it around myself instead. I sighed, my shoulders shaking with laughter that walked the line between irony and frustrated tears.

"Sorry for saying with 'w' word." I hung my head, cold water dripping from my still sudsy hair to patter against the waterproof vinyl covering my nudity. "It's just a figure of speech."

"Understood. But lamp regulations mean I must respond somehow when you use it." Ismail averted his eyes and extended a hand. "I won't take it seriously unless you say otherwise. However, it looks like you could use some help."

"I won't be using up a wish, though?"

"No, not for something so simple as a hand up." He smiled, though still not directly at me. I hadn't expected a Djinn to be so charming, mostly because all the stories seemed to be about the Seelie ones. Ismail was handsome, polite, and here to grant wishes. Also mysterious. I realized I knew next to nothing about him, and decided that should change. After I was decent, of course.

"Okay." I took his hand. He managed to haul me up, shower curtain and all. Plastic rings clacked together. Ismail's hand was warm and soft, especially after the unintentionally ice-cold shower, and it lingered on mine long enough for me to think getting back under the spray was a good idea. I shouldn't be having thoughts like this about a guy, not after a messy breakup less than two weeks ago.

"I'll leave you to finish bathing." He inclined his head in something like a slight bow. "If you need me again, just call." He vanished in a puff of smoke, thank goodness. My thoughts and feelings were all over the place, and I still had shampoo in my hair.

I stuck my head back in the shower to rinse it out. Conditioning would not happen today. I wasn't a polar bear shifter. I didn't want to put my whole body back in the arctic spray, and the last thing I wanted to do was fall down in there again. When I shut off the water, I tried to hang the curtain back up. Lost cause. It had torn, making it hang almost drunkenly with one corner skewed. At least I hadn't bent the metal rod on the way down.

Finally dry and wrapped in my robe, I headed back to my room to dress and call the people down at Facilities. They'd send someone with a new shower curtain and to check the water. They'd done the latter for me twice already this week, so I apologized for being a nuisance. After I hung up, I wondered why they had found nothing wrong with the pipes or the water heater before. But I didn't have time for that kind of woolgathering. Instead, I headed out to my first appointment.

My major wasn't all that different from others at PPC for the first couple of years, but this final semester of mine would definitely be. While I still had two courses in the classrooms on campus, the rest of my time was split between meetings with my adviser and the volunteer outreach sessions she'd set up for the other four people taking Extrahuman Social Services with me.

The weather was brisk but sunny, so I walked up Thayer and took a right on Angell Street and walked the six blocks to the senior center. I waved at the care aides and their charges. None of those were my clients. I set up in a side room with a small tea table and waited. Minutes later, Mrs. Donato shuffled in and sat across from me, crossing her ankles and pouring tea into a china cup so delicate it looked like an extension of her fingertips when she held it to her lips for a sip. Her file said she was a precognitive psychic, but I'd never heard of her predicting anything. The older Extrahumans tended to be more reserved about using their powers than the ones who came of age around the Reveal, or my generation.

We chatted as usual after I'd asked all the questions on my form. Mrs. Donato told me stories about the days when she was my age, back during what she called "the humans' civil rights movement." I paid attention, not to the tales themselves, but how she told them. I had to look for signs of dementia, like repetition, using the wrong word for something, or mixing up names. I didn't take notes while we spoke, a technique I'd been lucky to master quickly. Clients felt better about confiding in a counselor whose hands weren't busy recording. At the end of our time together, I bumped my purse with my foot and toppled it, sending lipstick, coins, and my wallet under the couch. I knelt to gather my things.

"Oh, dear," said Mrs. Donato. "Oh, my goodness me. Oh, I'm so sorry, Jeannie."

"Excuse me?" I looked up from stuffing everything back in my bag. Mrs. Donato peered into my empty teacup.

"Your leaves aren't good. No, not at all." The sigh that escaped her lips made the hair on the back of my neck stand up. She was making an honest-to-goodness prediction, all right. Why had I used loose-leaf tea that day? The last thing I needed right now was both of us getting freaked out by a scary premonition.

"Oh?" I hung my purse on the arm of my chair this time and got back in it, letting my conversation go back to the default mode I used with clients. "How's that, now?"

"The leaves here, they're telling me you've got an unlucky day in store for you." She lifted frail shoulders in a tiny shrug. "There's not much 'how' about it, though there may be a 'why.' You're a shifter, so you might not understand. I'm afraid it's entirely unavoidable, too."

"Well, thanks for the warning." I gave her what I hoped wasn't the lamest smile ever. "My day's over after two more chats like ours anyway. Hopefully, there won't be much room for bad luck to come get me while I study in my room."

"Whatever you say, dear." Mrs. Donato shook her head, then stood with the help of her aluminum cane. "Bye, now."

"Until next week." I smiled, hoping nothing in my voice or expression acknowledged her condescension.

My second appointment with Miss Agostino, a lion shifter, went well enough. She didn't make any weird predictions, anyway, although her nose wrinkled more than usual. She was generally ornery, being one of the older set who still thought shifters shouldn't mingle with Magi or tithed Faeries. Living in the PPC dorms meant I "smelled like magic" to her. I noted a slight decline in Miss Agostino's conversational patterns. Physically, she actually seemed to have improved. After our meeting, I made a note in her file about a new memory evaluation.

I waited almost twenty minutes before I realized my third and final client for the day wasn't showing up. I'd have to get out of here and head to his house. While I pushed the tea cart out of the room and down the hall toward the senior center's kitchen, the left wheel fell off. I sighed, wondering whether Mrs. Donato had noticed the loose wheel instead of actually reading the tea leaves.

While trying to snap the wheel back on the cart, I pinched the web of flesh between my thumb and forefinger, shrieking in pain. The wound healed almost immediately, a nice fringe benefit of being a bear shifter. And screaming like that had a fringe benefit of bringing help. Donna Murphy, one of the care aides, came running.

"Wow, I thought that cart looked shaky this morning. Mentioned it to the kitchen staff and everything." She made a clucking noise, then leaned over to jury-rig the wheel. "What do I need to do, give it a ticket and put a boot on it?"

I snickered. I liked Donna. She was one of the most experienced aides, with a snappy sense of humor and the ability to MacGyver things like the broken cart. I got up to give her some room but bumped the cart with my hip on the way up. The entire tea tray slid off the top of the cart, cups, and saucers tinkling in pieces on the hardwood floors. I reached out but missed the teapot by a centimeter. It hit the floor, going to pieces like a water balloon.

"Oh, now I'm teed off." The aide shook her bobbed dark brown hair out of her face. "Okay, maybe more 'teed on.'" The front of her scrub top was drenched.

Oh, Donna! I'm sorry!" I flared my nostrils but got no scent of blood. At least none of the broken china had cut Donna. I took a few steps back down the hall and opened the broom closet.

A long, wooden handle fell out and smacked me on the side of the head, stinging my dignity more than anything else. I bent to pick it up and got whacked in the back by the dustpan. All I could do was sigh and snag the cleaning utensils. Sweeping up the china shards wasn't easy, especially with some of them under the cart. But once Donna got the wheel back on, she pushed it forward so I could get the last of the mess. I dumped it all into a trash bin in the closet, then put out the sandwich-board sign to warn people about the wet floor until someone got a mop.

"*Piso mojado.*" Donna smirked. "Seeing that always makes me want pizza, even though I know it has nothing to do with cheesy oven-baked goodness."

"Seriously, in total agreement with you." I laughed. "But no time for pizza now. Have you seen Mr. Kazynski?"

"Oh, no, I haven't." Donna looked up the hall and then down it. "He actually hasn't been here since last Friday. Mitzi said something about a stomach bug, I think."

"Oh, okay." Everyone knew Mitzi, a crow shifter, was the senior center's biggest gossip.

"Guess that means you've got to take a walk, huh?" Donna peered down at her still wet top. "And I need to go change. Don't want to go through the rest of the day smelling like bergamot, or people might think I'm having an affair with Captain Picard. I'll tell the House staff about the spill so they can mop."

"Thanks, Donna." I pushed the cart more carefully, this time, getting it back to the little alcove next to the kitchen where someone would bus what was left on the tray. Then, I headed out the door and down the steps.

My first mistake was not taking a left when I was supposed to. I didn't realize my mistake until I got all the way to Lippitt Park and the border of Providence and Pawtucket. I turned right around and marched back the way I came, bumping a woman coming out of a coffee shop. One of the coffees on her tray fell right off, lid popping to spill black coffee all over my pastel pink and white dress. At first, I was thankful it was iced instead of hot, but it felt like wearing ice later. I apologized and gave her five dollars before heading on my way.

Finally, I got to Rochambeau Avenue, the street Mr. Kazynski lived on. His building was halfway down a steep hill, so I had to walk carefully as I silently scolded myself for wearing four-inch platform heels. I changed my internal tune when my right foot landed squarely in dog doo. In flatter shoes, I might have been splattered.

I stopped in front of Mr. Kazynski's building, hanging on to a fence as I tried to scrape the mess off my right shoe. I'd be mortified to track dog droppings into the old fellow's apartment. But the pavement was uneven. Scrambling to catch my balance on the fence, I felt something crack at the back of my left foot. I fell on my tail for the second time that day. What in the world was wrong with me? I wasn't a klutz normally, and there wasn't even a slippery shower with ice-cold water to escape here.

To make the whole culmination of public humiliation more complete, I saw curtains twitch on the first and second floors of Mr. Kazynski's building. Just what I always wanted, an audience. I shook my now sweaty hair off my face and reached into my handbag. I never went anywhere in platforms without a pair of ballet flats in my purse, or anywhere in pastels without a wrap dress right alongside it. And people wonder why ladies carry such big bags. It's for times like these, of course. For a bear shifter like me, those might happen even more frequently if I had to shift for some reason.

I couldn't change my dress, but the shoes were a must. I slipped the pumps off and replaced them with the flats, noticing a run in my right stocking, of course. On a day like this, what couldn't go wrong? I stood and sighed as I reluctantly dumped the platform pumps into a trash can. I had no choice. Not even a Faerie cobbler could fix something that broken.

The entrance was on the side of the building, so I walked halfway down the driveway and up the three steps to the stoop. The door buzzed, unlocking almost before my finger hit the doorbell. Mr. Kazynski had seen me coming, of course, but even though I should have expected the early buzzer, I didn't react fast enough to pull the door open in time. I rang again, he buzzed again. Finally, I got in.

"Miss La Montagne, good morning." Saul Kazynski's round figure took up most of the breadth of the doorway. He stepped back and aside, making room for me to get by.

"Good morning, Mr. Kazynski." I smiled, feeling like I could just about find the nearest patch of bare floor and go to sleep for the rest of the day. "I heard you've been home with a stomach bug, but we still need to have our visit."

"Yes, I know. Miss Murphy called while you were on the way over." He tilted his head, a scar at his jawline reminding me of all the stories he'd told about being a violinist over in Europe.

Instead of saying we ought to get started with the mandatory questions, I yawned. Mr. Kazynski shook his head and tut-tutted over me, offering lemon tea and jam on toast. My stomach rumbled in response before I could politely decline. I sat in his well-appointed but dusty parlor, watching him shuffle into the kitchen. The apartment was spacious but cluttered with furniture, curio cases, and nick-knacks. If Saul ever needed a wheel-chair or even a walker, he'd have to redecorate or possibly even move. I made a mental note to tell my Professor about this. It was the kind of situation that could make an illness or injury lead to a rapid decline for a man his age.

Saul was in his nineties, an Empathic Psychic, and an immi-grant. He'd come over alone, married and had children later in life than was typical, and set himself up as a violin instructor. He'd bought this building to house his whole family in. None of them had stayed. His paperwork said he had a granddaughter my age, but she'd moved out of Rhode Island the second she turned eighteen. Mr. Kazynski had lived alone since his wife died, and he'd retired from teaching music the year before we met. I was probably the only one who'd seen the inside of his house in all that time.

When he came back with the tray, I watched him, paying attention to his shuffling gait. He seemed steady enough. Like other people his age living at home, he had a system for navi-gating his living space that worked for him. I noticed there weren't any rugs or mats on the floors, and if there'd been door-jambs, they'd been removed. Someone had given him advice at some point, then. I didn't feel so bad about not visiting his home sooner.

He set the tray on the coffee table between us and served himself, leaving me to fix my own tea and toast. I started to give him a formal thank you, but he stopped me.

"Please, call me Saul, Miss La Montagne."

"Okay, Saul. And you can call me Jeannie."

It was as though some tightly coiled thing in him unwound. When he answered my questions, it was in a more relaxed fashion than I'd ever seen from him. When the conversation segued into the idly directed chatter I'd gotten used to, he stopped again.

"Today, Jeannie, I'd like to tell you a story you haven't heard."

He settled his teacup down on its saucer, then leaned forward on his easy chair. "But first, I must show you something." He unbuttoned his right sleeve and began rolling it up.

I looked on, realizing I'd never seen him in a short-sleeved shirt. I took a deep breath, steeling myself for what I'd always suspected but hadn't confirmed. Because of this, when he turned his arm out, presenting the number like a line of graying ants inside, I didn't gasp or show any sign of shock.

"You always suspected this, Jeannie." Mr. Kazynski was stating a fact, not asking me a question. "And I know why."

"Please, Saul." I shut my eyes, opening them again after a short enough time to excuse the expression as a long blink. "I'm not supposed to talk about my time in the Boston Internment with clients. I wish I could—"

I put my hand over my mouth an instant before thick blue smoke filled the space on the sofa next to me. I had turned my head before it cleared, taking in Ismail's thick eyebrows, drawn together on his brow as he opened his mouth to question me.

"Ismail!" Saul's exclamation startled all the imminent excuses out of me, and Ismail turned to face the old psychic. "How long has it been?"

"Too long, my old friend." The Djinn's gentle smile did nothing to hide the tears threatening at the corners of his eyes. "I thought I'd never see you again."

I acted on my first impulse, reaching out to grab Ismail's hand and give it a squeeze. His eyes widened when he turned his gaze back on me. Then, he looked up, down, around the room with his cheeks coloring, pulling his hand away. What had I done wrong?

CHAPTER FOUR

Ismail

No one had dared touch me since I took up service in the lamp. Everyone else had known better. Even my own wife hadn't, though I thought that had more to do with using the lamp to escape front-line combat than the volatile and fickle power an Unseelie magic lamp represents. Jeannie had made a wish, and I'd greeted Saul instead of addressing that. Anything could happen if I didn't act fast.

"Did you mean to wish for such a thing, mistress?" I forced myself to look at Jeannie, unable to mold my expression into anything resembling a smile. I felt the buildup of magical potential behind her wish statement deflate like a slow leak in a tire.

"No, Ismail. Sorry about that." She pouted, making me struggle not to look at her lips. "Figure of speech again. And I'm sorry to you also, Saul. I'm not supposed to bring people to our meetings."

"*Dobre.*" Saul shook his head, as though clearing it of the impulse to speak in Russian. "Enough about what you are and aren't supposed to do. You're a guest in my house, both of you. People visit so infrequently, and I won't let the college up the hill decide what we can and can't talk about in my home." He pushed the plate of toast and jam toward Ismail. "And you. I know you don't have to eat, but once upon a time, you liked to. Help yourself."

I looked at Jeannie. She blinked, and her lips parted as she realized just how much control she had over me and my actions.

"Wherever we go, Ismail, you can decide whether you want to eat or drink or, I don't know, even go get a haircut. I don't want you to wait for my permission for things like that."

It was my turn to drop my jaw in perplexity. This was the second such freedom Jeannie had granted me. It was almost as though she knew what it was like to be enslaved herself. But she wasn't a Djinn, nor a Faerie of any type. What's more, she was a woman living in a western country in the twenty-first century. If Saul were my master, I'd understand this sort of behavior. From someone like Jeannie, it made no sense.

"Yes, mistress," was all I could say. I poured a cup of tea and took a triangle of toast from the plate.

"I was about to tell Jeannie a story you already know, Ismail." Saul took up the conversational manner I remembered from the boat on the way over from Europe. The grin he wore wasn't exactly the same. It had a drawn and worn quality. Even time spent working while starved hadn't added to it back then.

"Oh?"

"Yes. About the rescue you mounted and its true purpose."

"It was never my rescue." I sighed. "Wilfred wished you and your fellow prisoners free." Instead of gasping as I expected, Jeannie grew even quieter. Her nostrils flared, and her brows drew down in thought.

"Yours was the face I saw at the window, yours the hand that cut the wire."

"I know, Saul. But if men doing evil excuse themselves by saying they were following orders, I can't claim goodness for doing the same."

"You can't tell me you wouldn't have broken down the walls of that prison on your own, Ismail. I won't believe that of you."

"I can neither confirm nor deny that for you, old friend." If dehumanization hadn't broken Saul Kazynski's belief, I surely wouldn't. "But perhaps this isn't the kind of story to tell a young woman."

Saul glanced at Jeannie, then looked down at the number on his arm. He rolled his sleeve down and closed the button at the cuff after only a few tries. He locked gazes with me, the depth of his stare trying to convey something to me, or maybe his intention was the reverse, to take some thought or feeling from me. Saul was an Empath, the kind of Psychic who held sway over feelings. The more emotional the state of the surrounding people, the more he could sway them. He'd never been harmless, and especially not now when age had given him wisdom and experience despite his continued lack of restraint.

"I disagree, but understand how it might be awkward to hear tales of heroics you don't believe you participated in." Saul stood more easily than his age should have allowed. "I can do better than that for my guests." He turned and shuffled over to a sideboard with a music stand beside it.

I knew what I'd see before he opened the weathered case, so I watched Jeannie instead. This time, she did gasp. The inside of Saul's violin case was embossed with the seals of both Faerie Monarchs, meaning he was one of the few mortals alive who'd been honored by both the Goblin King and the Sidhe Queen. Such a reputation gave him benefits many would envy, including the fact that his violin couldn't be destroyed. Even if it were shattered, the instrument would rebuild itself if the majority of the pieces got returned to the case. The enchantment was eternal as long as it remained the property of his blood relatives.

The music Saul made felt like it sent hooks into the very fabric of my heart. I'd thought it coated in steel until Jeannie's demonstration of compassion when I first appeared in the apartment. I swallowed as if that would banish the tears from my eyes. Then, I looked away, out a window, so neither of them would see how affected I was. But I already knew it was no use as far as Saul was concerned.

The whole reason he and the other prisoners at the German camp had remained alive long enough for Wilfred to find them was Saul and his violin. Empathic Psychics each had a talent, some art form with which they wielded their power to bend hearts. Every afternoon for nearly a year, the SS Commander wrote up orders to terminate all the prisoners come morning. Every evening, Saul played for the soldiers. Every night, the Commander tore up the papers that would doom the camp's denizens. I can't imagine the things Saul Kazynski had seen, heard, and endured in that year. I didn't want to. But his music wouldn't let me ignore my pain anymore.

Beside me, Jeannie seemed just as appalled and enthralled as I was. I wondered why, and when I tried to tell myself it was none of my business, Saul's music wouldn't let me. Maybe Jeannie thought her responsibility as an old man's caregiver meant she shouldn't trouble him. I was a Djinn, even more than that, her servant for the time being. I finally understood why she was so awkward a mistress. She was accustomed to being the one serving. Having someone else at her beck and call must be difficult for her.

As the notes spiraled out of Saul Kazynski's instrument, I understood that I hadn't done nearly enough. The time in the lamp had artificially extended my life, but I'd done nearly nothing with my extra time but sit and mourn. I'd gone about business as the lamp required, even though Unseelie rules meant I had so much more potential to act than that.

Wilfred Harcourt had been an opportunist, Kimiko Ichiro

desperate. Jeannie La Montagne was an altruist. She couldn't think of real wishes because she wanted to make them count for others, not herself. Whatever crucible she'd been through as a youngling had forged a will bent on action and accountability. If all masters of Djinn since the beginning of our time in lamps had been like her, we'd live in a utopia.

I made a vow to myself. Jeannie La Montagne thought she didn't need wishes or even help. She was wrong. I would do everything in my power to help her until I couldn't anymore.

CHAPTER FIVE

Jeannie

Saul's unexpected performance left Ismail dumbstruck beside me on the loveseat. Me, not so much. The notes pouring like audible honey from that amber violin set my skin tingling with goose-bumps. I didn't recognize the piece he played, but whatever it was had me wanting to get up, get out, go and do some good in the world, even more than my usual days entailed. The city was full of people struggling, hopeless, suffering. I'd helped a handful turn that around during my nearly four years in Providence. And I had to do better before I graduated and went back to Boston.

I could. I had Ismail. Three wishes, but I didn't understand the potential scope of his power. I'd need more information, some from researching magic lamps, but the rest from what I did best. Ismail would tell me. What was it Olivia had said? Unseelie Djinn had flexibility, loopholes, allowances built in by the Goblin King that would let him talk things over. After a hundred years inside a lamp, I'd be going nuts, wanting to chat nearly all day once I could. But Ismail didn't seem to share that trait. I'd need some confirmation and knew just where to get it.

When I said goodbye to Saul Kazynski at the door to his apartment, Ismail vanished himself instead of walking out with me. That sort of thing wouldn't do at all. I headed up Camp Street, this time, not wanting to retrace the unlucky steps I'd taken on the way here while going back to campus. Once back at the dorm, I washed up and changed into something more appropriate for the stomping around College Hill I'd do later. After that, I headed down the hall to knock on a door.

An orange origami paper dragon and a brown corrugated cardboard cutout bear rampaged across a construction-paper backed collage of buildings and shoreline. Each of them had a little crown made of Wrigley's wrappers. Scrawled across the bottom of the dorm door decor were the names Bobby and Blaine plus the tag-line "Team Tinfoil, blasting off again!" Neither of them had written that, but I didn't recognize the handwriting. I shrugged, then knocked.

"Come back in an hour." Even through the grumbling, I recognized Blaine's voice and the old movie quote. I chuckled.

"Housekeeping," I squeaked. "You want towel?"

"No towels, need sleepy." Blaine sounded more alert and also closer to the door.

"No sleepy." I gave up on the quotes since they'd done their job and gotten his attention. "I need some Tinfoil help."

"Oh, fewmets." I heard a rustle of fabric. "Hold on a minute."

I tried not to stare when Blaine Harcourt opened the door, but that was nearly impossible. There were just too many things going on in that doorway. He was in a set of Slytherin pajamas, eyes red and dragon-pupiled. I still wasn't used to seeing him with short hair, and he had a brunette girl in a yellow and black dress clinging to his waist, peeking out at me from under thick bangs. I recognized her.

"Kimiko, good to see you again." I tried not to smile because I knew most girls younger than me were reminded of Barbie dolls when I did.

"Yeah, nice to finally meet when we're not getting shot at and other unfun things." She giggled but looked up and down the hall a few times.

"Um." Blaine blinked, his eyes going back to their usual brown. "So, were there noise complaints or something?"

"Oh, no, nothing like that." I chuckled, watching Blaine's shoulders drop as the tension went out of them. "It's just that we have a mutual acquaintance who I'm not sure how to handle. And I wanted to ask if you'd chat with me about him."

"Ohmigod, Blaine!" Kimiko put one hand over her mouth. "She means Ismail!"

"Wait, what?" He rubbed his chin. "You mean your Unseelie Djinn? The one who paid respects to my stepdad with a stupidly rare antique?"

"Yeah, that's the one." I shrugged, knowing I couldn't possibly look nonchalant while blushing. "Can I come in?"

"Okay!" Kimiko bounced on her toes, shouldering Blaine out of my way. His lips made a grouchy frown, but his eyes twinkled. When I'd run into them in Newport, I hadn't thought they could seem more complementary to each other. I'd been wrong.

Blaine gestured to Bobby's desk chair. I sat, watching him toss the sheets and blanket back over his bed. He collected a tablet and sat down, tapping it to wake it up. Kimiko sat on the edge of the bed, dangling her bare feet off it. She smiled.

"So, Ismail the most introverted Djinn in the known universe, what do you want to know?"

"Introverted?" I blinked. "He pops out every time I say the 'w' word."

"Woah, really?" Blaine scratched his head.

"Yeah." I glanced from him to Kimiko, wondering why she hadn't been the one to answer. "What is that, weird or something?"

"Oh, yeah, it is." Kimiko twisted her hair between her fingers, then tapped the beige tips against her other hand. "He came out to talk to me twice. Like, he avoided doing that whenever he could. It was so bad, half the kids at The Academy thought his lamp was either empty or fake."

"But there's no such thing as an empty magic lamp." Blaine scoffed. He tapped the tablet a few times.

"Yeah, well, The Academy isn't selective about who it admits." She rolled her eyes. "So glad to be transferring here this summer. Anyway, those were all the students who didn't know better."

"Yeah, I almost forgot those lamps need an inhabitant, or they cease to exist." I took a regular-sized breath and counted to five. If they didn't stop going off on tangents, I might lose my patience. "But we're talking about Ismail in particular, not magic lamps in general."

"Oh, sorry." Kimiko dropped her hair. "Well, Ismail's pretty formal, except when he's not. He told me a couple of things, like how he'd been in the Harcourt hoard before when part of it was back in London. That was before Wilfred married your mom, Blaine. And also, he has kids. He gave me advice like only people with kids can, and when I called him on it, he said I sounded sassier than his son, but he'd let it slide because I reminded him more of his little girl."

"Well, Wilfred hasn't lived in London since the 1940s." Blaine sighed and bowed his head. "Hadn't." Kimiko threw her arms around his neck and leaned her cheek against his.

"I'm sorry, Blaine."

"No, it's okay. I'm just not used to thinking of any dragon shifter I've met in person in the past tense." He blew a smoke ring. "Anyway, you might think that means Ismail's from the 1940s, but he's not. I saw him on Mourning Day. His clothes are Turkish, from the turn of the twentieth century. Djinn can make their clothing look different with Faerie glamour, but I was in dragon form when I saw them. They were authentic, not magic.

He must really be that old. And he was from a wealthy family, too, judging by his token of respect."

"Wait, you said he was in Wilfred's hoard, then the Academy, then you took the lamp?" I chewed on my lower lip. I wasn't Lynn Frampton or anything, but I wasn't stupid either. "So I'm the third master of Ismail's lamp. That means, when I'm done, he needs someone to replace him."

"That's going to be hard for a guy who's been locked up in a magic lab for decades. If he doesn't find one who's a tithed Faerie and get them to agree, he's stuck in that lamp forever." Kimiko's jaw clenched. "How many wishes did you make?"

"None." I shook my head. "Can't think of anything worth it, you know? It has to be something that'll have maximum impact."

"Wow, Jeannie." Blaine squared his shoulders. "If I thought you were a different kind of person, that'd be scary to hear."

"Don't mind the big paranoid ticklish dragon." Kimiko poked Blaine in the ribs until he snickered. "I totally understand. Even though Ismail's other weirdly un-Djinn trait is being helpful, I had a tough time deciding what to wish for too until I was in the moment."

"I bet he's not going to mind if you take your time deciding, either." Blaine tapped his tablet a few more times. "He wouldn't have the resources or knowledge to try to track down his family in the modern era, but I don't have that problem." He untangled himself from Kimiko. "I'll head to the library and look into it between classes. It shouldn't be anything too dire if you can't even think of stuff to wish for."

"Okay, but before you go, I wanted to ask Kimiko a couple more things."

"Sure!" She smiled. "Go ahead."

"Do you have any idea what he likes to do for fun?"

"Wow, hold on." Kimiko twirled her hair. "Um, no. All he mentioned was *choreg*, some kind of bread, I don't know. Oh, and he went nuts when he saw me drink kefir while I couch-surfed back in January. He said something about not believing it was sold in so many stores."

"Okay then, good to know." I nodded. "Thanks, you guys." I got up. "You're both super helpful."

They got up, too. I'd almost forgotten Blaine was heading to the library, and he almost forgot to change into regular clothes instead of his pajamas. I heard Kimiko ribbing him about that particular instance of absent-mindedness as the door shut behind me. After that, I almost walked out of the dorm, thinking I'd bring some kefir back from Whole Foods and then ask Ismail to talk, but then I got a better idea. I headed back to my room, got his lamp, and put it in my handbag. Then, I went out to Hope Street again, paying attention this time.

I had the perfect idea to try to help Ismail come out of his literal and figurative shell. All I could do now was try it and see what happened. I headed down to Kennedy Plaza and took the bus to Cranston. Not having a car in Rhode Island was way more inconvenient than it was in Boston, but public transportation was my jam. In the middle of the day like that, the bus wasn't crowded. I got a seat in the middle and pulled out my phone so I could read an eBook.

Picking up where I left off in the story that distracted me during the end of Spring Break in Newport was a little jarring. I'd picked out something gloomier than usual, a real tear-jerker. I couldn't keep reading it. Maybe I was as done with being down on myself as I'd been with Dale when that girl showed up. Donesville, capital of Alldone County.

In a month and change, I'd be one of the first shifters to graduate from PPC. I'd do it with honors and had several job offers all over New England from Extrahuman Social Services organizations, even without a graduate degree. I might be a bear shifter, but I'd risen from the ashes of the Boston internment camps like a phoenix. In three more years, my cousin Bobby would follow in my footsteps, just with a different major.

After visiting Mr. Kazynski's, I was absolutely sure Ismail was a survivor, even if I didn't know of what yet. He'd understand, and hopefully even be inspired to do something with his life after the lamp. During that bus ride, I had full confidence Blaine and Kimiko would track him down a replacement. I also thought Ismail was just like one of my clients, except in a younger-looking body. Now, I look back on the Jeannie La Montagne, who'd ridden the Cranston bus that day as a shortsighted ninny.

I had no idea what I was getting into.

CHAPTER SIX

Ismail

I knew Jeannie brought me along with her out of the dorm, downtown, then on the bus. But I had no idea why. I waited after she stepped off the intermittently stopping vehicle, pacing as she walked along a street somewhere. I could have checked our location, listened in on the surroundings, but I didn't. Long habits thicken like tree trunks. The more seasons they grow, the stouter they get. But when they fall, the more space they leave, and the impact with the ground is impossible to ignore. All I had going for me as a lamp-bound Djinn was the predictability of my power. The last thing I wanted was to risk losing it. Wherever she was going, whatever she meant to do, had my nerves spooked like a green colt.

The door Jeannie walked through squeaked, bells ringing with its movement. I could have guessed what kind of place this was, but the aroma gave it away entirely. I stopped pacing with one foot in mid-air. Fresh-baked sweetbread, not exactly like what I'd smell on the streets during celebrations, but close enough for climate and water source to excuse the difference. But what was a bear shifter with a French surname doing in an Armenian bakery? She'd stopped moving, too. I listened for her voice, thinking she'd be ordering something by now. But she didn't. I wondered what she was waiting for.

"Ismail?" Jeannie didn't whisper. I imagined she wasn't even trying to hide the fact that she was talking to her handbag. I didn't answer, a tactic that had worked with Kimiko. It hadn't with Wilfred, but Jeannie was a mundane shifter. She didn't have magic or much knowledge of how Faerie worked. If I kept waiting, she might even put herself in debt to me by asking thrice.

My face heated, my shame like wildfire. Who was I to take advantage of someone like her? She'd devoted her life to helping people when others would turn away. Maybe I'd done the same thing, but my so-called devotion came with being nearly indestructible and halted aging. No job could pay her like that. I put my foot down, closed my eyes to focus on modernizing my clothes, and took a deep breath.

"You called?" I opened my eyes as the smoke of my vanishing cleared. Either I'd put myself closer to her than I'd thought or she'd moved when I appeared. I tilted my head down, wondering whether her bear form was proportionate to her human size. I couldn't help but smile, imagining a petite bear. The air being filled with that sweet bread scent helped my mood even more.

"Yeah." The brilliance of her smile made me take a step back. I wasn't used to being smiled at like that, or at all, really. As I was wondering whether Jeannie had any notion of what personal space meant, I felt my elbow knock into something that wobbled.

The shift in gravity meant I didn't have to turn around, but I did anyway. A snap of my fingers righted all the cans, jars, and plastic-wrapped packages that threatened to clatter and shatter off the shelf. I blinked when I saw the labels had words in both

Armenian and English. And then, I got a good look at where we were.

One-half of the space was a small specialty market selling various goods with import labels. The other half had a counter, tables, and chairs, and that's where the delicious bread smell came from. I didn't glance back at Jeannie but knew she watched as I looked around. I took a step toward the counter, peering up at the wall behind it to read the menu there. Foods I'd dreamed about but hadn't seen in decades were all on offer. A setup to the right of racks and rows of bread promised real coffee, the way I'd taken it before getting bound to the lamp.

I had to close my eyes, take a few deep breaths, clench my jaw. To say my feelings were mixed was like declaring the grass is green. Anger that someone who barely knew me would presume I'd want a reminder of lost days warred with relief at being surrounded by familiar sights and scents. Underneath that, an emotion I didn't recognize had taken root. Whatever else I might think of Jeannie La Montagne, I had to acknowledge that she'd brought something to my numb existence. What that was, whether it meant good or ill, remained to be seen.

"Do you like it?" She stepped to my right and stood beside me. "I'm sorry if this isn't right. We can go somewhere else."

"No. This is perfect." It was, too. A perfect storm of memory and the surge of thought that went with it. I'd weather it. It was more than what I deserved for abandoning my family.

"Okay, then." Jeannie's voice was light, but I knew she could tell I brimmed over with an emotion other than joy or even plain old happiness. "Why don't we order something, then sit down and talk?"

She didn't take my hand as she had in Saul's apartment. My fingers twitched, inappropriate. Even without the tether of joined hands, I let her lead me to the counter. The middle-aged woman behind it smiled, clapping floured hands when I greeted her in Armenian and made an order. She waved us at the seats, promising to bring everything over once it was ready. In moments, an aroma of coffee more plush than the carpets in my lamp permeated the store.

I gestured to the chair across from the one I stood behind. I shouldn't pull it out, or Jeannie might think this was a date. Lamp-bound Djinn shouldn't get emotionally invested in their masters, a mistake I'd had trouble avoiding the last two times. But none of that made any difference to Jeannie. She sat, beaming up at me as though I'd presented her with all the trappings of a modern romantic outing. I settled into my seat, folding my hands on the table in front of me.

"Why did you bring me here?" I studied her face, waiting for an explanation.

"Okay, that wasn't what I was expecting." She leaned her head on one of her hands. "I figured you could use some time out of the lamp. Someplace that's not as crowded as anything near campus. You're welcome."

"You do realize that once you make your wishes, you're not likely to see me again."

"That doesn't matter to me." Her eyebrows pulled together.

"I don't want you to waste your time."

"That's nonsense." Jeannie smirked. "You just want to hide in your lamp and avoid everyone. But you're going to have to get used to the outside world someday."

"Not likely. Or don't you know what happens when a Djinn has no successor after the lamp's third master?"

"Oh, I know. Eternal servitude." She nodded. "But that's not happening. You'll have one."

"How?"

"You should realize that Kimiko Ichiro thinks she owes you one. Blaine Harcourt, too." She smirked. "They're working on tracking down your family."

I froze, letting that sink in. The Tanuki and the young dragon shifter were both intellectual forces to be reckoned with. As a team, they'd surely find something, a fact that had me trembling. Jeannie tilted her head, lifting her hand as though about to reach across the table. And then our order came.

The smiles that stretched our faces felt tied on, like banners over a rained-out garden party. Sensing the tension, our hostess set everything down and made herself scarce. I gripped the edge of the table instead of a fork or my coffee cup, knuckles whitening. The fear that sang through me made no sense. But that was the worst part about anxiety. It robbed me of reason as surely as bandits ransacked unsuspecting travelers.

"Make them stop." The words came out low and soft, sibilant, reminding me of prayer more than the demand I'd intended.

"I'll do no such thing." Jeannie leaned on the table, reaching across on my left past the plates of pastry and the coffee things. Her fingertips brushed mine. "Anyway, no one could stop those two once they get into researching something. You're stuck with being helped. It's hard to accept, but that's what happens when you do things for other people. They want to return the favor."

"But I had to help Kimiko. Exactly like I have to help you." I shook my head, unable to move my hand away from hers. "I followed orders. She doesn't owe me anything."

"All the same, she thinks differently. Ismail, don't try to tell me you only do what's required." She locked gazes with me. Would it be dangerous to look away? That generally got shifter's hackles up. I stared back, not willing to chance it.

"Very well. I'll stop protesting their efforts. But you know the big flaw in the Golden Rule, right?"

"You're talking about that whole 'do unto others' thing. No, I don't. Tell me."

"It doesn't take into account that one man's trash is another man's treasure. And the reverse is also true." I imagined kicking myself. Why couldn't I just say right out that I feared to find any relatives I might have after all this time? I should be able to admit how what they might think of me was more paralyzing than a staring contest with a cockatrice.

"You'd rather be forced to live at the whim of whoever coincidence directs to your lamp than meet long-lost relatives, then." She nodded, withdrawing her hand, then picked up her cooling coffee and took a sip. "You're going to find this hard to believe, but I understand." She broke eye contact.

"You can't, possibly." I sighed, staring down at my *choreg*. Leaving it on the plate felt like a parallel to the rest of my existence since that day in the desert when I'd acted too late. Denial.

"You're not my client, or not officially, anyway, even though what we're doing here is exactly the sort of thing I'm devoting my career to." She picked up her fork and knife and began cutting a corner off her sweet bread. "Because we're not on the books, I can tell you about the Boston internment camp, how my family should have been able to get away before the round-up, and why they didn't. It was my fault, you see. If you want to know more, just ask. I'll tell you anything you want to know about that. You don't have to tell me why you'd rather not meet whoever they find. But it might be easier for you to accept if you dip your toe in the idea before it happens. I won't bring it up again. Just remember, I'm here if you want to talk."

I stared, finally unable to stop myself from gaping as she put the fork to her lips and took a bite of *choreg*. How could Jeannie La Montagne sit there enjoying herself, treating her senses to a delicacy I'd denied myself for a century? Maybe she did know I could have treated myself to a glamoured version of *choreg* at any time while in the lamp. But what uncanny instinct could have told her I hadn't? It was like she could literally see how I felt, like Saul.

"Are you Psychic?"

"I get that question all the time." She smiled around the mouthful of bread, then swallowed it and went to work cutting off another piece. "Not really. My grandma was, so I have hunches sometimes. Anyway, you ought to eat some bread before it gets cold. And have some coffee, first."

Ignoring her about the coffee might have looked like an immature act of rebellion. It wasn't. I had to know whether I could handle an outing like this before she tried to rope me into another one. I didn't bother with a fork and knife, letting my hands get sticky as I lifted the bread to my mouth.

At first, I'd worried the bread and company while eating it would take me back in time, sting with the sense of empty tables and sorely missed faces. It didn't, or at least not quite. Every time the flavors on my tongue threatened to whisk me away like a cyclone, the clink of metal on Jeannie's plate anchored me to the present. No one in my family had eaten their *choreg* with a fork. It was time to call her bluff.

"I want you to tell me." I picked up my coffee cup, the sticky heat on my fingertips making my mind wander to what it might be like to reach across the table, pick apart the rest of Jeannie's bread, and feed it to her by hand.

"Hmm?" She paused with her knife about to pierce the crusty, seeded hide of *choreg* again.

"The Boston Internment." I sipped, the brew frothy and bitter. It was time to hear a tale of the sort of survival I'd run from enduring, time to look the sins of my past in the face and stare them down. "Tell me everything."

CHAPTER SEVEN

Jeannie

"Okay, then." I set my fork down, laid the knife aside. With one hand, I turned my water glass in a circle, then took a deep breath. "You know how the Reveal happened, right?"

"I know the version they teach at The Academy."

"Then you know enough about that." What a relief. "Good. About a year after all the chaos, Registry laws went into effect. They started registration, getting a database together of all the Extrahumans. The Magi and Psychics did it freely for the most part. When you can hurl fireballs or make people forget you exist, having people know what you are isn't such a big deal. Most of the Faeries felt the same, especially the Seelies. They like their rules, and there's always the Under to escape to. But it was different for shifters and vampires, some of the Psychics, too."

"I remember overhearing a conversation about Psychics denying their abilities during the Registry. Something Kimiko spoke about with a Psychic vampire?"

"Oh, that'd be Henry Baxter." I smiled, remembering how good an influence he'd been on his girlfriend Maddie since they got together. "Yeah. They did. It's how they managed to help some of the most vulnerable Extrahumans survive the Reveal. But they could do that because there isn't a way to test a Psychic except by what they say. Only the Summoners are really noticeable. But anyway, that's not something shifters can get away with. There's a physical test for that, scientific, where they take a sample and know what we are in under a minute, no matter how sneaky we're trying to be about it."

"Did many shifters try to hide, though?" Ismail tented his fingers around the little coffee cup, gazing into it before taking another sip.

"Lots, especially in the southern half of the country." I stopped spinning my water glass, then dried my fingers on the napkin in my lap. "There was a ton of intolerance and backlash down there back then. My cousin Bobby's parents took off and lived out of a truck in the Ozarks for three years. But Boston was different, like most of the Northeast." I sighed. "Or so we thought."

Ismail stilled, reacting to something. I glanced around, trying to figure out what it could be. Tithed Faeries sensed all kinds of magic, so there could be danger nearby. I flared my nostrils and tilted my head, trying to scent or listen for any threat. But there was nothing. And then, I noticed his eyes were locked on me. Something about me or the story I told had alarmed him. I should have known. He was another survivor, after all. And now I understood the real reason an Extrahuman Social Services worker shouldn't talk about her personal troubles with clients. It wasn't for privacy, but so we wouldn't cause more harm than good.

"Are you all right, Ismail?"

"I will be." He set his coffee down in the saucer, then put his hands on the table. "Please continue."

"Okay." But I wasn't sure I could. I closed my eyes. "What

should I tell you about first? How we thought it was perfectly reasonable for the Mayor to ask all the shifters to move into temporary housing on barges in Boston Harbor? How about when he had a Boston PD task force guarding us for our own safety? I was seven and thought the police were our friends, just like I'd been taught. We were like frogs in a pan on a slowly heating stovetop, and then we were like fish in a barrel."

"What do you mean?" Ismail had leaned forward until he was on the edge of his seat. He didn't blink, something I thought was impossible for anyone but dragon shifters.

"I mean there wasn't much we could do when people on the barges started disappearing. But my mom and dad had some ideas. They started a resistance, teamed up with some otter and walrus shifters. They snuck out and contacted Kelpies and Selkies. With that much Water magic, we would have been able to defend the barges and also find out where the missing people went. It would have been the first time since the Faerie Wars that many from both sides worked together too. Mom and Dad had what seemed like an ocean of hope. They thought for sure we'd get the lost shifters back."

"You didn't, of course." Ismail tilted his head, his steady stare interrupted by a sheen of tears and one long blink.

"No. The Kelpies and Selkies never made it. The Queen didn't want her people to help. She stopped them instead."

"But why?"

"She refused to risk her Selkies, so she locked them all in the Under until the Internment was over. Even worse, she put up a Ban to keep the Kelpies out. Without them, half the Extrahumans on the barges disappeared before the President sent the National Guard to stop the Internment."

"How did she find out, though?"

"I told her, of course. That's how it was all my fault." I shook my head, hiding all traces of guilt from my face by picking at the napkin under the table instead where Ismail couldn't see. "I sent her a message in a bottle, dropped it off the side of our barge. Because I thought she'd help us."

"Her decision is hardly your fault."

It was my turn to sit still. The napkin I'd let go of fluttered to the floor, and for once, I didn't lean down to pick it up. And just as he had earlier, Ismail turned his head, scanning the room for threats. I studied his face again, noticing things I hadn't the first time I'd seen him in Newport. Faint lines marked the corners of his eyes and the space between his brows and traveled the breadth of his forehead. The jet curls just above his ears mingled with scant silver strands. They matched what I saw in the mirror every morning, adornments etched by guilt and the yarn of penance spun from my life since I squealed on my parents.

Ismail didn't ask how I was. Instead, he retrieved my fallen napkin, placing it on the table between us like a white flag or a peace offering. He left his hand beside it instead of drawing away again. He waited until I met his eyes again, then turned his palm up. I reached across and took his hand, not caring about how it was still slightly sticky from the *choreg*.

"Well, now you know the worst thing I've ever done. Thank you."

"For what? Surely you've told this story before."

"Yes, I have. But no one I've told it to so far extended their hand to me afterward like you just did." I squeezed it. "So, thanks."

"I still wonder one thing." He looked down at our hands, then squeezed back. "What happened to the missing people?"

"You remember how I said we thought the police were protecting us?"

"Yes." He nodded once.

"There actually was a threat. Extrahuman trafficking." I took a deep breath before continuing. "Many of the families on those barges were found later in circuses, zoos, mines, factories, tourist attractions. Some of them were even okay afterward. But the rest they only found records of. Laboratory records. And ashes. Can't forget those."

"I'm sorry." Ismail reached across and placed his other hand over mine.

"You shouldn't be." I sniffed, shaking my head as the corners of my eyes leaked. "You couldn't have done anything."

"I should have asked Wilfred to pass my lamp to someone else."

"You were in The Academy by choice?"

"Yes." Ismail's grasp loosened, as though he expected me to pull away. "I didn't want a second or third master for my lamp. I wanted nothing more to do with people anymore, Extrahuman or not."

"I understand." I knew what he'd have to say to that. Even though no one else I'd shared this story with ever made it this far, I'd been where Ismail was right then. I had to decide how much I wanted to tell him.

"How could you?" He blinked. "What happened next for you was the opposite of my— well, I guess you could call it a life. But you devoted your life to helping others after making that mistake."

"Because I wanted to curl up and hide." I closed my eyes, taking a leap of faith in this Djinn I'd only just met yet felt like I'd known forever. "I had a whole plan about heading up to the Arctic circle and just hibernating until I didn't wake up." I kept my eyes closed, expecting the worst, since that was what I'd told him.

Ismail let go of my hand. I heard the scrape of the chair on tile as he stood. I tried not to listen for his footsteps, but my enhanced hearing got nothing, anyway. He'd Vanished himself, then. I knew I shouldn't tell anyone but a psychiatrist about contemplating suicide. I'd gone and scared him off like a jerk after promising to help him.

"Yes, you do understand." His words startled my eyes open.

He sat beside me, in the chair he'd pulled around the table. "I'm sorry for doubting you, Jeannie."

My mouth dropped open. I could hardly believe he was apologizing to me when I'd gone and been inappropriate. He put his elbows on his knees, then folded his hands and leaned forward and gazed into my eyes. How had I failed to notice his, how they were brown but shot through with amber? Was that a Djinn thing? Why did I care about something like that when I'd decided to treat Ismail the same way I would a client?

But I hadn't been the same with him as with Mr. Kazynski or Mrs. Donato. Ismail wasn't like them even though he was technically older than either. He looked my age even though his mannerisms were from a different era and he talked like a high-society Harcourt. I wondered what he thought of me, but didn't dare ask, not while we locked gazes like this.

For once, I wasn't sure what to do or say. Usually, I was the one to break the ice or help people shake off their shock and the inaction that went with it. I thought back to catching Josh Dennison and Nox Phillips snogging in the dorm laundry, how I'd moved them along and given Nox a place to stay. Instead of the usual snickering that memory inspired, I got chills and shivered like it was December instead of the end of April.

Ismail reached out, pushing a lock of hair aside that had fallen out from behind my ear. His touch lingered as his fingertips brushed the side of my ear. Maybe it was an accident, maybe something else. His gaze was intense, penetrating. I'd spent the entire afternoon trying to get through to him so that I could help, and now he sat beside me, looking at me like a desert traveler might gaze at a glass of water. I knew I was looking at him exactly the same way. This kind of thing had happened to me before, but it had been one-sided. I took a breath again, trying not to prepare whatever words might come out with it and just speak to him in the moment. But the words didn't make it in time.

"Did you enjoy your *choreg* and coffee?" The woman from behind the counter shuttled our empty plates from the table to a large round tray.

"Very much, thank you." Ismail turned his head to smile at the woman. Had he smiled before this? I couldn't remember because that expression looked so natural on him. Familiar too, like I'd seen it before somewhere. I definitely had. Where, though? It was right on the tip of my brain but took off like a tomcat leaping down from the top of a fence.

I sat in silence, collecting my thoughts as Ismail chatted with the woman about *choreg* recipes in Armenian. She handed him a coupon card, the kind where you collect stamps each time you visit to exchange for a discount later. She'd filled half the spaces up for us already. After that, she faded back into the duties of running the cafe and left us to each other's company again.

"Would you walk with me for a while, Jeannie?" Ismail had stood and extended his hand to help me up. I took it, but couldn't take him up on his offer.

I explained that I had a meeting with my adviser and then a class. When he asked when we could talk again, I gave him a time later that night after dinner. His smile was the last thing to vanish as he went back into his lamp. Even though the bus back to Kennedy Plaza passed by some lovely spring scenery, all I could see was that last smile. It had touched his eyes, genuine.

CHAPTER EIGHT

Ismail

The only place a Djinn could go for advice besides whoever his master trusted was either his Monarch or the Under. Technically, that wasn't true. I couldn't leave the lamp unless she called me out of it, but I could communicate with anyone I knew who was in the realm opposite this one. I stood in front of the silver-backed mirror on the north wall of my lamp and willed it into a window. After that, all I had to do was imagine Neil Redford, and he'd appear on the other side of the glass—as long as he wasn't in the earthly realm, at least.

"Well, I'll be a monkey's uncle. Ismail! How you doing, old buddy?" Neil flashed his perfect teeth. Perfectly white, that is. They were sharp, almost like a shark's, double row included. Seeing any Faerie in the Under meant you got the real them without their glamour. Redcaps all had teeth like that, plus pointy ears and gray skin. I could also see Neil's mantle, the sign of rank in the Goblin King's Court.

"You've moved up in the court, I see." I smiled back. "Congratulations."

"I'd say thanks, but really you ought to compliment my son, Fred." Neil turned his smile down to a grin. "If he hadn't helped me fix the King's cleaning contraption, I'd never have made it past Marquess to Duke."

"Well, I'm glad you're not still a Page after all this time" I'd met Neil because that's what we both were during that first year and a day in the Under. Neil had been a pioneer on America's western frontier, but in the other realm, mortal nations and geography didn't matter. I'd been sent to help him out there on occasion. Only one thing divided Faerie, the rift between the King and his counterpart.

"Well, shoot. Has it really been that long?" He shook his head, a forelock of sandy blond hair streaked liberally with gray flopping over one of his gleaming red eyes. "You don't look like you've aged a day. But then, you've been in a lamp all this time, right?"

"Right."

"That's a bum deal, buddy."

"It has its bumless moments, however." I smiled and gestured at the opulent surroundings behind me.

Neil threw back his head and laughed. No, he guffawed. I had to wait nearly two minutes for him to compose himself again and by then his knees were sore from slapping. Watching a Redcap laugh would have been sheer terror for most mortals, but I wasn't one. Even though the insatiable maw he'd opened could have devoured my lamp, items ensorcelled by the Monarchs persisted. Because I'd tithed to the King, no Unseelie creature could truly destroy it. I was another matter entirely.

"So, you've been in there all this time. You didn't call, you didn't write, you didn't Magic Mirror your way over to see me." Neil narrowed his eyes. "Why?"

"I was tired." I shook my head. "Shell-shocked. That sounds like what you'd call yellow-bellied, I know."

"Now you look here." Neil set his jaw to the point where it was squarer than I'd thought it possible for jaws to get. "You've seen two wars up close and personal, and a couple of gunfights besides. These days, they call what had you in its teeth PTSD. It's serious enough to get any fighting man an honorable discharge. I won't hear you calling yourself yellow-bellied over hiding again."

"Fine. How about if I call myself a coward for agreeing to the lamp life to begin with?"

"I always thought you did it to protect your family."

"I wish it were that simple."

"Well, shoot." This time, Neil didn't laugh. "So why chew the fat about it with me now, after all this time? You join Alcoholics Anonymous or something?"

"I thought Prohibition ended eighty years ago?" The quip came automatically, with no wind in its sails. "As to why, I met someone important."

"Woah now there, Izzy." Neil's hands went up like he'd been outmatched on a dusty Main Street at high noon. "What did you do, meet another Djinn through this magic mirror thing like some kind of Under dating service?"

"No. And I think you've got the wrong idea. Maybe." I tried to shake off the memory of Jeannie's hand in mine. "I met my lamp's third master."

"Let me guess—you have no idea where any of your descendants are, or whether any of them are tithed."

"Correct." I didn't need to explain to Neil that I was facing eternity in this lamp.

"Does this new master know?"

"Yes, and it's not good. She's taking her time with wishing, and she wants to help me track down my family."

"Well then, how's that bad?"

"I don't know. It seems like it shouldn't be, but for some reason, I just can't shake the idea that something's not right."

"So is it the situation or the lady who's giving you that there case of the heebie-jeebies?"

"The lady is one of the most altruistic people I've ever met. It's the situation." I took a deep breath, figuring bluntness would be best. "I sense coincidence at work here."

"Shi—" A gong sounded somewhere off in the distance on Neil's side. He waited until it rang thirteen times. "Look, I gotta run. Duke duties over at formal court with His Majesty. But just so you know, it's not just you. Coincidence has been flapping its butterfly wings all over Providence for months now. We'll talk some other time, but I'm gonna give my oldest kid Fred a heads up. He'll have the time to help you out over the next week or two. Who's your master lady so I can put him in touch?"

"The bear shifter, Jeannie La Montagne, from Boston." I studied Neil's face, which had gone uncharacteristically blank and chalky-pale under the gray.

"Noted. You'll hear from him tonight. He's got some friends with time most of the rest of us don't have. They'll fill you in." My old friend was in such a hurry that he turned his back before the mirror had silvered back over.

I gazed into it at my own face. I wondered how anyone could see it as the face of a friend, let alone more than that. My wife and I had met and married years before either of us had any idea how little mettle I possessed. Once Yeva found out, she'd grown dissatisfied and shrewish. I'd made it worse by proving her right when I failed to confront her about it. Was my inaction truly this PTSD illness Neil had mentioned, or had it started with the wife I'd failed to protect?

I wasn't sure I wanted to find out, but I wasn't sure I had a choice.

I felt the pull of Jeannie's attention less than an hour later. My earlier indecision had me rethinking the whole thing. Maybe I could endure eternity in the lamp better than facing my past and trying to convince a stranger to take a potentially life-ruining turn in here. But that wasn't what I actually feared at all. The worst would be to find none of them were left at all, that there were no descendants, that Yeva had died to protect children who wouldn't survive to have their own someday. A close second would be to find them and discover they hated me.

"I wish I didn't have to do this research paper." Jeannie's statement made it impossible not to appear. I sighed, changing my clothing's appearance to the modern-looking t-shirt and jeans. The lamp's magic Vanished me into a scarred wooden chair beside a long table covered with papers and books. I turned my head to see her with one hand clapped over her mouth.

"That sounds like the least genuine wish I've ever heard." I almost covered my own lips after that utterance. My time talking with Neil had left my guard down. I placed my hand on the table, not wanting to reveal more than she'd already seen with that one slip.

"Good. I don't want you to actually grant it." Jeannie shuffled a few of the papers, some marked with a red pen. "This is the second draft. Third time's the charm, and at the rate I'm going, it'll be done early. It's easy enough, just mildly annoying busywork."

"You ought to be careful, though, with these fake wishes." I shook my head. "Even though I'll agree not to grant them, coincidence has a way of hearing."

"Silly Djinn, coincidence isn't sentient." Jeannie's giggle was soft enough not to anger the librarian, but still, it caught his attention.

"That may not be true." The librarian sauntered to the end of the Reference desk closest to us. "Since you're not in a major course of study which includes magical theory, I don't expect you to know that. But I thought you might benefit from some enlightenment on the subject under your specific circumstances."

"Thanks, Mr. Waban." I raised an eyebrow, startlingly intrigued by Jeannie's reaction to public correction.

"You can thank me by keeping that in mind later." As the librarian turned away, I noticed his eyes had slitted pupils, dragonish, confirming my guess about his identity. He'd been on the Frontier, too.

"So, Jeannie, if you didn't want me to complete your research paper, why did you call?"

"Fred Redford wants to talk to us. He's meeting us here after his class gets out. But first—" She turned her head, looking up at the cold gust of wind from the opening library door. "Well, they're here. I don't have to tell you."

"Hello again, old man." Blaine Harcourt sat down across from us, followed by a woman who definitely wasn't Kimiko Ichiro. This girl looked the same age as the other, but that's where the resemblance ended. She was slightly shorter, had a more generous figure, and tawny hair framed her smirking face. "I brought some extra help."

"Hi, I'm Lynn, A.K.A. Darth Sarcasm, A.K.A. the Tinfoil Brainiac." She grinned at me and winked at Jeannie. "You didn't tell me your Djinn looks more like Aladdin than a big blue guy. Nice. High five!" Lynn raised one hand, holding it up halfway across the table. Jeannie blinked, then reached out and slapped it.

"It's good to meet you, Lynn." I nodded, hoping I wouldn't have to slap the high five. She spared me the exercise. I looked at Blaine. "Jeannie told me you and your mate were doing some research. What did you find?"

"Not much yet, although there's a new lead." Blaine took a deep breath, then let it out with three smoke rings. He glanced warily over my shoulder at Mr. Waban. "We found out that your son went to Poland and your daughter to Italy. We lost track of him, but it seems she got married to a man from America. The problem is, Ellis Island naturalization did some funky things with people's names. I'll let Lynn take it from here."

"Yeah, okay, so…" She pulled her long hair over one shoulder, then pulled out her phone and put it on the table in front of her. "We didn't find any records of Armenians coming over from Italy, just Italians. But there were a bunch of women who came over with brand new husbands, married in Italy instead of stateside. A ton of them had no maiden names, just the names of the towns in Italy where they got married. And half of them were called 'Monalisa' which just means 'milady' in Italian."

"We'll have to go through all those records in more detail." Blaine leaned over, peering at Lynn's phone. "There are loads like that. We have to cross-reference some magical records, too, but we need to ask you a couple of questions. This might come down to genetics instead of records."

"Very well." I crossed my arms over my chest, instantly regretting the unconscious gesture when Lynn raised an eyebrow and nudged Blaine in the ribs.

"Okay. We know you're Faerie, born a Changeling. How far back is your family line as far as Faerie blood goes?"

"As far back as anyone can remember. Djinn mostly, but my grandmother's side was Sidhe all the way back."

"Okay, good. We'll look through the magical records for an immigrant with that kind of lineage. If your daughter was trying to find a match so she could come to America, she might have said that up-front and center. Magi families back then looked for that kind of thing. Might be hard if she married a human though." Lynn jotted something in a small notepad. "So, how about your wife's family?"

"Shifters, though she wasn't one." I closed my eyes. "Leopards. Kimiko told me they're almost endangered now."

"Wow, I'd love to look at a sample of your blood sometime." Lynn's eyes were wide. "Oh, sorry. It's just that we're working on

Extrahuman genetics this semester. I'm an Alternative Therapies major."

"Our Lynn here is going to be a doctor." Blaine grinned.

"So's Jeannie, technically, if she goes to Grad School." Lynn winked. Jeannie didn't. She was looking past Lynn at the door again. "What's wrong?"

Jeannie didn't say anything. But when Blaine glanced over his shoulder, I knew there'd be some kind of trouble for sure.

CHAPTER NINE

Jeannie

A sudden pang of guilt got replaced with annoyance as Blaine Harcourt got up and left when Tony Gitano walked into the library with Fred Redford. The whole business over Spring Break had changed Blaine's attitude about lots of people, places, and things, but not as far as Tony the cat shifter was concerned. That was a shame in my book. I wasn't alone. I caught Taki Waban, the new librarian, shaking his head with a soft clucking sound.

"Fracking dragon shifters and their paranoid tempers," Lynn muttered as she shuffled the papers into a loose pile and dumped them on top of the books in her backpack. She looked over her shoulder as she headed for the door Blaine was tapping his foot next to. I saw her mouth a word that could only be sorry in Tony's general direction. She couldn't know the crazy local rumors about Tony's family or the fact that he was here on a full scholarship. Blaine might, but probably didn't care. He could be a snooty little jerk sometimes.

"Hey, Jeannie." Fred smiled and waved as he greeted me in library-appropriate tones. His mouth tilted sympathetically. "Eww, research paper. This is why I went with Engineering. All my research is math."

Ismail chuckled at that. I glanced over at him, wondering whether he'd gone to college back in Armenia and what he'd studied if he had. I'd have to ask him sometime.

"So's half of mine." I lifted one sheet after another of notes I'd been taking, flipping one over with each word. "Lies. Damn lies. Statistics."

"Oooh." Tony leaned over, peering at the numbers and their labeled columns upside-down. "This is the opposite viewpoint paper? Not looking forward to that one next year."

"Yeah." I shrugged. "It's a descriptive paper, mostly, with just a short survey this time. But it's a distraction, so I want to get it done quick. I'd rather be doing more of my clinical work." I raised an eyebrow at Tony. "You're taking Extrahuman Psych Research next year?"

"It's part of what they decided should go into my crazy major." He shrugged, not really looking at Fred or me. Tony got dodgy every time something unique about him came up, and I just happened to know he was pioneering a brand new major here at Providence Paranormal. The Headmistress herself had mapped it out for him.

"Okay." I didn't want to piss him off or freak him out. "You guys need help? I could use a break from this."

"Actually, that'd be awesome." Fred grinned. "We need a few books that aren't in the Nocturnal Lounge. It's for an Extrahuman History paper."

"Yeah, and after we get them, we're going back there." Tony looked down at his shoes. "To the Lounge, I mean. Because you never know when it will get knocked over, blown up, or set on fire again. Same goes for this library."

"If any of that happens, we'll fix it." Fred waved a hand absently as though Tony's remark was a gnat.

"I'll stay here and keep an eye on your things, Jeannie." Ismail gestured at the heavy bag I'd just zipped my draft and graphs into.

"Thanks, Ismail." I smiled. Fred nodded at the Djinn, almost like he'd expected to see him there. Before I could wonder what was up with that, Tony took a step back, looking for all the world like someone had dropped him headfirst into a room full of rocking chairs. "What's wrong, Tony?"

"Are you a Seelie Djinn or an Unseelie Djinn? And don't try pulling anything lame, like trying to tell me you're Dorothy Gale from Kansas." Tony wrinkled his nose.

"Unseelie. Not that it's any of your business." Ismail narrowed his eyes, looking scary for the first time since I'd met him. "And if you'd like me to hold my tongue about what you are, you'll stop asking me personal questions."

It was only then that I realized Ismail was at least as dodgy about giving answers as Tony, possibly more. One of these sides of him must be something rarely revealed. The cat shifter backed down, not exactly seeming to relax, still on guard. Ismail gave him a look that reminded me just how much magic power Djinn tended to pack, more than most professors here on campus. Taki Waban's presence probably did more to deter Tony than Ismail's, then again maybe not. If it were me on that end of this confrontation, I'd be more comfortable with the dragon I knew than the Djinn I didn't.

Fred cleared his throat, then handed me a slip of paper with some titles on them. I headed into the stacks without consulting the computer or the library ghosts. Fred probably asked me for help because he knew I had some firsthand information about his subject from more than a few of my clients. I stopped at a shelf near one of the back windows and stood on my toes. There they were, barely touched dust-jackets gleaming. I pulled two books down.

"There's one more on the top shelf, but you'll have to get it." I shrugged. "I can't reach that one." Ironic how I turned into a half-ton bear but stood just under average height in my human form.

"Thanks, Jeannie." Fred ran his finger along the spines until he got to the book he wanted. He slid it off the shelf but lost his grip. I started to raise my hands, but it'd be too late. That book was going to hit me right in the face. I'd be lucky not to have a broken nose.

And that's when Ismail decided to make another smoke-filled appearance. Tony coughed. Fred gasped. I waved the smoke away from my eyes to find out what had happened. The Djinn stood there, wearing the clothes I'd last seen him in two weeks ago. The blue jacket made his gold sash and vest stand out, the red scarf around his neck creating an even sharper contrast. I'd forgotten how striking he was, and the guilt from earlier came back with a vengeance. He glanced down at the cover of the book he'd plucked from the air over my head.

"The Boston Extrahuman Internment," he read aloud. "Are you sure this is the right book?" Ismail handed the book to Fred. And then Ismail was glaring at one of the most easygoing Redcaps I'd ever heard of.

"Of course, he is." A flash of embarrassment raced through me, making my face burn with a flush. I didn't keep it a secret, the fact that I'd been there. I didn't advertise it either. "He wants to talk to me for a History project. It's nothing I haven't done before."

"So, how about it, Jeannie?" Fred didn't exactly look at me. I knew he was about to do something awkward. Then, he surprised me by looking me in the eye when he asked. "Do you have time for an interview?"

"Time, yeah." I nodded, suddenly so weary I could have gone back to the dorm and slept for sixteen hours. In my Freshman year, I'd talked to what felt like hundreds of other students, answering their questions about what it was like on the barges and whether we knew the human government would go that far before it happened. But then, those students published their papers. Instead of interviewing me directly, they started citing those older interviews to the point where I hadn't done one all year. Fred might be the last undergrad at PPC to interview someone who'd actually been there. It was completely unnecessary. There had to be some kind of ulterior motive.

"So how about it? Will you come down to the Nocturnal Lounge and answer a few questions? I can promise you the pizza's good." Fred sighed. "I hate to ask, but..." His shrug was shallow and half-hearted, but at least he didn't look away. The Redfords were stand-up people, even if they had been a little muddled with Gitano Gang business in the past. That was what decided me.

"Sure. Just let me grab my bag." I headed back through the stacks faster than I'd intended, leaving Fred and Tony behind. I tripped over my own feet, but Ismail caught me by the arm. He'd managed to keep up, shooting a final dirty look at Tony as he went.

"You talk about this freely with your classmates?" Ismail put his hands on the table, leaning down to try to look at my face as he spoke. I wondered whether that was a Djinn thing or just him.

"Not all of it, but yeah, I answer their questions for their papers and projects. Been doing it the whole time I've been at this school." I held the shoulder strap of my bag longer than I should have, staring at it for a moment. "Why would I stop now?"

"Because most people don't speak of times like that unless they have to." His brow furrowed.

"Well, I do." I sighed. "Have to, that is. If people like me who were there don't talk about it, people might forget how it happened." I turned away from him as I snagged my sleeve in the zipper on my backpack. I sighed and fixed it. His expression had been flat, mask-like. I glanced at his un-glamoured clothing again. I wondered exactly how long had he been in that lamp. What had he been through to make him like being locked in a vault?

"You're a brave woman, Jeannie La Montagne."

"Thanks, but I hope you don't mind if I disagree. It's just talking. Come along and listen, considering you already know the worst part of that particular story. I promise an Unseelie Djinn like you will fit right in at the Nocturnal Lounge."

"Oh, wow." Fred interrupted. I almost chewed him out for it. "Yeah, he totally will. Henry's going to love this guy. Did you know that he saves people from falling objects, too? And hey, I didn't catch your name. I'm Fred Redford." He stuck out his hand.

"I know. I am Ismail." The Djinn bowed instead of accepting the handshake, then raised an eyebrow as though he expected some other reaction from the Redcap.

"Cool." Fred scratched his head as though he was trying to think of something. Then, he bowed back. "We'd better hurry or we'll lose Tony."

He was right, too. I caught a glimpse of the cat shifter's trench coat as he headed out the door. We hurried after him and, of course, I tripped over my feet a few times in the process. Ismail caught me every time. It was only a few blocks away, but the entrance to the Nocturnal Lounge was partway down a creepy old trolley tunnel. I didn't mind walking down there with three other people but watched for Ismail's reaction. He seemed nervous at first though his eyes twinkled merrily when Fred did the secret knock to get the door to open.

I'd been in there before, but it had been almost two years since the last time. And I wasn't sure what to expect after the renovations over Winter Intersession, but they managed to make it almost the same again. I'd almost forgotten how many books were crammed into the mezzanine and how just about everything edible floated through the air in the hands of the ghostly

Skeleton Crew. True to Fred's word, there was heavenly smelling pizza downstairs in the area upperclassmen had nicknamed The Pit. Fred shooed me over to a table already occupied by a dark-skinned Goth girl I thought I should recognize and Nox Phillips, a Kelpie one year behind me. Nox was mated to Josh, an Alpha wolf shifter who led the most diverse pack on campus. I sat at the far end of the table from them, not expecting much in the way of conversation.

"Hi, Jeannie." Nox picked up her coffee and moved to a seat next to mine. "So, Fred convinced you to show up?"

"Yeah, I don't like saying no to interviews about Boston unless I really have no time."

"Good, because after he asks his questions, we have a few things to talk to you about as well." The Goth girl had moved over, too. I peered at her, trying to place the name that went with the face.

"I'm Maddie, Lynn Frampton's roommate up in 566." She touched her chest and mumbled a few words in what sounded like Latin. "It's okay that you don't remember me. I'm an Umbral magus."

"Oh!" Memories flooded back from other times I'd met her. "Okay. You have an amulet that's helping me remember you now. Your parents are vampires, and you're from Vermont."

"Uh-huh." She gave me a cheery smile. "Hello again!"

"Okay, so now that's done." Nox grinned. "You're about to graduate, so you know what an Extramagus is."

"Oh, no. I mean, yeah I do, but they're like the baddest of bad news."

"The worst." I'd almost forgotten Ismail was there, standing at my right shoulder.

"You know, I always thought that was kind of biased. I mean, I can think of lots of people with big power who did the right thing most of the time." I chewed my bottom lip, not wanting to rehash my stance from almost every class that mentioned Extramagi but also not able to justify blanket fear and anger for an entire classification of people.

"Yeah, we know how you feel about stereotyping." Tony sat down with a cup of black coffee. Instead of drinking it, he pushed it over to Maddie. "That's why this is going to be hard."

"What's going to be hard?" I blinked. "I thought Fred just wanted an interview."

"Nope. He just thought that was the best cover for bringing you here. Convincing you all your recent klutziness and weird coincidences are because an Extramagus has his or her eye on you is what we're really after." Nox sighed. "I have to admit, it took me a while to believe it myself when it happened to me. But don't you wonder exactly what kind of trouble I was in back in February?"

"No, I don't." I shook my head. "I figured it was all about the Faerie Court conflict."

"Which got kicked up by the same Extramagus the lot of us think has been messing with the school for a long time." Nox ran a hand through her hair.

"That's disturbing, but it makes sense." Ismail sat down between Tony and me. "My last master thought one was causing her problems."

"Bingo." Maddie tapped her own nose. "That'd be Kimiko, and she was right. She and Blaine were lucky to escape with their lives. If you were her Djinn, then you know something about what a mess they were in. Nox already told you she and Josh were targets. Before them, it was Henry and I and before that, Bobby and Lynn."

"Whoever it is, seems to target two people at a time, folks who are either powerful or assets to the school, the community, or both." Henry Baxter, wearing an old black leather jacket, sat next to Maddie. "You two fit the bill."

"But Extramagi are so rare." I shivered, wondering why this felt like some kind of intervention. "I mean, there's a registry now. Everyone's accounted for, and there aren't any Extramagi on the books in Rhode Island anymore." I looked at Henry. "Not since you got turned, right?"

"We figured you'd say that." Maddie pulled out a tablet and tapped it twice to activate it. "That's why we talked it over with Josh. He gave us the okay to tell you about pack business, so we brought you this." She pushed it across the table at me.

The app running on the tablet looked like an interactive flowchart. Dates and names stood out, some of them instantly familiar. Tapping a listing gave a description of an event, sometimes a reference link to a public record, article, or book title. I'd almost been there for several of them, and others looked suspiciously like excuses I'd heard from a specific group of students. I might be blonde, but I wasn't dumb.

"Tinfoil Hat." I stared at Nox. "So that's the reason your whole pack even exists. You really think an Extramagus is after you guys?"

"Worse than that." Fred pushed a plate with one slice of pizza in front of me.

I picked it up and took a big bite, my stomach rumbling. Ismail cleared his throat, and Fred tossed another slice from his huge pile of bread and cheese to my plate. I might be petite in human form, but bear shifters got hungry, and my metabolism meant the calories burned up before they went to my hips.

"How could it be worse than all this?" I gestured with my free hand at the tablet. "I mean, most of you almost got killed, for crying out loud."

"We think the big bad is after the school, trying to get it shut down." Maddie tapped one of the entries. I saw an article about the arrest of Doctor Brodsky the Summoning professor in January, charged with two deaths. Then, she moved on to the Obituary for Wilfred Harcourt. "And he doesn't care who dies in the process, either."

CHAPTER TEN

Ismail

The conversation at the table went silent, although that didn't stop the Redcap Changeling and Jeannie from finishing their meals. That there was an Extramagus in the area wasn't news to me. I'd heard Kim and her mate, Blaine, discussing it, after all. But I hadn't realized this many people, an entire pack of shifters and others no less, were involved. I'd just assumed that, since Blaine Harcourt was a dragon shifter, he'd keep his troubles to himself. My servitude to Jeannie didn't require me to help her on this, or anything she hadn't explicitly asked of me. But an Extramagus could become the worst kind of tyrant. If left unchecked, they'd do anything to increase their power and lifespan or pay any cost. After that, there was no stopping them.

"I'm under no obligation to the rest of you or the school, but how can I help?" I leaned back in my chair.

"We didn't ask you here so you could help." Tony stared into his coffee. I gazed at the freakish aura of magic surrounding him.

I'd never heard of a magical feline shifter before, and normal shifters didn't have magic energy unless someone else put it there. So I wondered whether he could be trusted considering the group was up against an Extramagus. But then I noticed that Tony's magic came from Faerie. Before I could scrutinize it further, he shot me a glare over the rim of his cup. I had to stop looking at a member of this pack that way or risk them all distrusting me.

"Okay, so why did you want to talk to Ismail, then?" Jeannie brushed crumbs off her hands and crossed her arms over her chest.

"You know how we said you're a target?" Fred swallowed his second-to-last mouthful of pizza, then frowned down at his plate.

"Yeah?" Jeannie tapped her foot under the table.

"Like Henry said, there's always been two." Tony shrugged. "We think Lamp Man's the other one."

"Seriously? An Extramagus would target a lamp-bound Djinn?" Jeannie scoffed. "That's insane. All they do is follow orders, and you can't get at them when they're in their lamps."

"No, it makes sense." I sighed. "I helped Kimiko and Blaine more than I should have. Being Unseelie means I can bend some rules while doing my job."

"Let me guess: that's the closest you're going to get to telling us exactly what you did to piss the bad guy off?" Tony's stare reminded me of a bristling tomcat.

"Wow, Tony. Just wow." Jeannie stood up. "You bring me over here, lay something this big on me, and then insult my friend?" I blinked at that. I was used to dealing with frightened folk, masters or people who wanted to become one. Did she consider me a friend? "Don't think that I'm soft because of how I look. Oh, and by the way, you're not one to talk about being cagey."

"She does have a point, Tony." Fred managed to speak coherently around a mouthful of pizza. "You're a pretty dodgy guy."

"Yeah, about my own personal life which is strictly my business and none of yours. I don't mince words about this." He slapped his hand down next to the tablet between Jeannie and me, then stared at me. "This is serious trouble, people. We're trying to figure out who this Extramagus is before an innocent man gets executed for crimes against Extrahumanity. A Summoning professor was Mind-controlled for crying out loud. What else can this bastard do? We don't know. They're always one or more steps ahead of us, and we still have no idea why anyone would want to mess with the school. Mark my words, it's about something much bigger than making students and faculty look bad."

Tony was right even though I refused to admit that out loud, after his outburst. I had to move the conversation along to something constructive. Heading off the potential social eruption with a question would be the best course. Luckily, I had plenty of those.

"Is there a list of the powers you think this Extramagus has?" I looked at the tablet, wary of touching it. I'd never used such a device before and wasn't sure how not to ruin their display.

The Umbral girl navigated to a different screen. I saw a few lists and scanned them. The rest of the information looked like a police dossier. I read that, too. When I shuddered, all eyes fell on me. I reminded myself that this was a group of students, young people with limited experience and without extra power from a lamp to help them. Neil had mentioned the older generation not having time, but I wondered whether he knew how dangerous this Extramagus might be. Right after that, I wondered whether I was overreacting. I composed myself, pushing down evidence of the cowardice that shaped my life when I was their age.

"How theoretical is this limitation you have listed for him?" I pointed at one of three guesses, careful not to touch the screen.

"Blaine, Lynn, and Olivia are our brain trust." Nox tossed her head. "They're the ones who checked into it. And Kimiko's the one who originally thought of the idea. You tell me how reliable she is."

"If his only limitation is being unable to use magic outside of Rhode Island, I'm not sure how you'll ever find an identity or a way to stop them." I sighed.

"Ismail, I wish to know who this Extramagus is." Jeannie pointed at the screen. There was no mistaking what she meant. I closed my eyes, focusing my magic like a drawn bow. But when I tried to loose it, send the bolt of my magic out to obey her command, it stopped.

"I can't grant that wish." My eyes flew open.

"Wait, what?" Jeannie's eyes widened. "I thought Djinn had huge cosmic powers but itty-bitty living space."

"The latter is true, the former not so much." I gestured at my face. "I went into the lamp when I was young. After tithing, but only weeks after my full year was up in the Under. And I got out at the same time as your father, Fred." I nodded at the young Redcap. "Also, I'm only a Marquess. Most Djinn are Dukes. I'm not as powerful as I could be."

"But what about the power from your lamp?" Henry scratched his head. "All the experience you have from however many years you've been in there? If it's a memory problem, I might be able to help."

"No need." I sighed. "I remember everything, including part of that extra power I mentioned before. But even a Djinn has limitations. For example, I'm limited in certain Faerie magics by my rank in the King's Court. In this case, something is blocking me, and the fact that I can't obey a direct command from the lamp's master tells me a few things."

"So, dish." Nox gave me a lopsided grin. "What's the four-one-one?"

"First, the energy blocking me is Faerie magic. Second, it's Seelie." A chorus of gasps sounded out around the table. I waited as they regained enough composure to silence their surprised murmurs. "Finally, the Extramagus is warded against Djinn. Do you understand what that means?"

"Ugh. It's right on the tip of my brain." Maddie put her head in her hands. "I'm not Lynn or Trogdor, and Olivia's asleep." She looked up again, peering at the rest of the group. "Anyone else?"

"Another Djinn." Nox tightened her hands into fists. "One in the um, other Court. The Extramagus must have one of his own."

"He definitely did when my dad had to rescue Blaine." Fred clenched his jaw, which was probably scarier for the others than me. None of them had worked with Redcaps in the Under, after all.

"But look here." Henry had slipped a glove on his right hand. He used it to tap the tablet's screen. "Kimiko made a note about how she thought all her wishes were countered by the Extramagus's own Djinn."

"Well, she *was* the one in the thick of that particular fight." Nox leaned her chin on her hand. "She must know what she's talking about there. But something about that explanation's not sitting well with the ancestors." Nox leaned back, rubbing her stomach and tilting her head as though listening to voices only she could hear. Kelpies got water magic and the ability to change into a horse, but that came with the input of anyone else who'd ever worn the pelt which gave them their magic. It seemed Nox was at peace with them, so their influence was probably a good thing.

"Of course, your ancestors are all riled up." Tony shook his head. "Kimiko was wrong. The drive-by shooting wasn't a Djinn wish; it was an Organized Crime hit. You don't need to make wishes for the big cat Mafia to shoot at Yoshi Ichiro's daughter. He's crossed them too many times in the courtroom."

Tony stood up. "Yeah, the Extramagus probably still has the same Djinn who knocked Blaine out over the Pell Bridge. But it's way more likely we've got a rat in Tinfoil Hat. Because the other thing that can ward against Djinn is a Monarch. Someone's carrying tales to Her. And I bet more than half of you right here think it's me. Probably for the best if I make myself scarce. Arrivederci."

Tony turned his back on the group, stalking down the length of the mezzanine. He looked back over his shoulder once. Directly at me, of course.

"He's been a real bag of cats lately," said Henry. "Don't take it personally."

"But he does have a point about a possible informant in or around your pack." I raised an eyebrow, intrigued that the vampire had brushed off the theory Tony had presented.

"Maybe, but that's for Josh to decide. He's the Alpha." Henry shrugged.

"Yeah, and he'll consider your opinion and mine as far as that goes, too." Nox stopped rubbing her stomach. "But I can tell you all right now, I think he's altogether wrong. And the Extramagus still has a Djinn on the line for a wish."

"Yup, I agree." Fred grinned. "And I bet it's for the same reason, too."

"You both saw something?" Jeannie looked from Nox to Fred, then back again.

"Yeah. Faerie magic energy surge." Fred winced. "I bet the only reason Ismail here didn't get any backlash is because of the wards we have here in the Lounge against that other unmentionable kind of Faerie magic."

"Is your whole school warded that heavily?" I blinked at Jeannie. "Surely there are students from the other side of the Under here."

"There are, so it isn't. They have their own Lounge. Spectral Magi and some diurnal shifters use it as well." She chewed her bottom lip. "I don't know how strong the overall school wards are, but they got increased after this Lounge and the library got wrecked."

"Is that why you have an ancient dragon for a librarian?" It was my turn to be bewildered.

"Wow. He's that old?" Nox shook her head. "I never knew. So many things make sense now." She chuckled. "No wonder Blaine's scared of him."

"Speaking of Blaine," Jeannie said, "shouldn't we bring him in on this now that Tony has left the building?"

"Nah, too late for him and Kimiko. Probably you guys, too."

"Don't dragon shifters need less sleep than the rest of us, though?" Jeannie glanced at Henry. "Well, besides our friendly neighborhood vampire, of course."

"Usually, yes. But he told us earlier that he has a big fancy dress formal shindig to go to tomorrow night." Nox wrinkled her nose. "Josh and I have to go, too, but I have time for a nap in the afternoon, and Blaine doesn't."

"Oh, no!" Jeannie shot out of her chair, putting her hands to her face for a moment. Then, she whirled and grabbed her bag. "I've got to go get some sleep, too. Sorry guys. Thanks for the heads-up, but I'll have to help you with it some other time."

"Wait!" Maddie reached out, tugging Jeannie's sleeve. "This is totally a life-or-death thing. It's not about you helping us, it's us offering to help you. I can hide you for a few days or something."

"Thanks, Maddie. I appreciate the offer, but I just can't take it." Jeannie somehow managed to look weary and frantic at the same time. "But the reason I have to jet is life or death, too."

"What do you mean?" Fred blinked.

"That hoity-toity costume shindig Blaine's going to." She turned to go as though that answered the question. When she scanned our faces, hers fell. "Look, you don't understand. It's a charity ball to benefit the Senior Center. I have to go and support it as part of my capstone class. If I miss it, I won't graduate. And even worse, the Senior Center's offerings could get cut if we don't raise enough. All those elderly Extrahumans would lose things like free medical screenings and temporary housing. I have to do my part."

I expected protests, but there were none. Maddie nodded, bouncing her dark curls. Henry shook his head and sighed, but grinned anyway. Fred's lips tightened, and he gave her some kind of salute. Nox stood up and shook her hand.

"Four of the pack will be there if you need us." Nox put her hand on one of her bony hips. "We're all rooting for you. Good luck, Jeannie."

But good Luck would be in short supply, as it turned out.

CHAPTER ELEVEN

Jeannie

"No way, Mom!" My fist hit the mattress so hard I dented a spring. "I'm not going to a formal event that my graduation depends on with Dale. Don't you remember? We broke up." I'd forgotten the morning of the ball was the same as Mom's weekly phone call from home.

"Well, I know that, Jeannie. It's a shame, really. I mean, he's such a catch." She sighed. "And stop grinding your teeth, dear. Those don't always regenerate so nicely if you crack them, you know."

"I shouldn't have told you." My finger hovered over the disconnect button on my phone.

"Well, of course, you should have, I'm your mother." Mom's airy tone clashed with that nasal Boston accent I'd struggled so hard to exorcise. "If you can't tell your own mother about breaking up with your high school sweetheart, who *can* you talk to about it?"

"I wish you'd maybe have some regular priorities for once, Mom." I took her bait instead of hanging up, flopping on my back and flinging my arm over my eyes like the long-gone Emo teenager I used to be. Thank goodness for speakerphone. "I mean, seriously. I'm not like you, holding one of her man's hands while he throws money at his love children with the other." As usual, she ignored my insulting outburst.

"All the same, if you hadn't dumped him, you'd have a date tonight." She clucked more like a chicken shifter than a bear shifter. "Going alone to functions like these is bad form. I'm not wrong about that."

"Madam." Ismail's voice made me jump clear off the bed and over to the other side of the room in an instant. "Miss Jeannie La Montagne does not have to attend her function alone this evening. Just before your call, I asked her to accompany me. I still await her reply."

"Oh?" Nothing but the distant sound of church bells came from Mom's end of the phone after that. I imagined the temperature dropping in her immediate vicinity. "And you are?" Her frosty tone confirmed my musings.

"Marquess Ismail, centennial Djinn in His Majesty's Court." Ismail grinned and dropped me a wink. "If you check your mailbox, you will find my calling card, including my regrets that I can't pay you a proper visit until after the event in question."

I stood there with my back against the dorm-issue bookcase with my mouth hanging open. Formal-manners Ismail was way more impressive than jokey first-meeting Ismail, and light-years more intimidating than coffee shop confessional Ismail. His entire manner was authoritative, commanding. There was no way my mom didn't know which His Majesty he was talking about.

"Well, Marquess Ismail, I certainly hope you know what you're getting yourself into with my Jeannie." She tittered exactly like she had in the one recording we still had of her high school graduation. "She can be a handful."

"I can assure you that your daughter is exactly who I want on my arm at such an important event." One corner of Ismail's mouth turned up slyly. "The senior center was renovated by one of my dearest friends, Duke Redford. And the work Jeannie has been doing there this semester is invaluable. The chance to ask her is almost as much of an honor as the acceptance I hope she will grace me with."

"Well, of course, she accepts." Mom sounded positively breathless. "I mean, you're saying yes, right?"

"I'd go to a cleanup in Roger Williams Park if Ismail asked me to." My cheeks hurt. I hadn't been aware of smiling that hard. "So, yes. I'm Marquess Ismail's date this evening, Mom."

"Thank goodness. You've finally taken your mother's advice for once." She chuckled. "Have a lovely evening." The phone let out three low beeps when she hung up.

"Oh, no! I used a wish!"

"Not technically." Ismail handed me a notecard, the kind that folds over from top to bottom. The paper felt almost velvety. I opened it and read the words inked in delicate, flowing script.

"It's an invitation to accompany me dated yesterday. But why?"

"I heard you speaking to your friends about the ball, of course." He shrugged. "My intention was to leave it on your desk so you'd see it after breakfast, but..." He gestured at the dark screen of the phone.

"But I don't have anything even remotely appropriate to wear! Everything I own like that is back in Boston, and there's no time to drive up there and get it." I hoped that didn't sound like whining. If it did, Ismail didn't seem to mind.

"You have a Djinn. You always have something appropriate to wear while I'm around." He grinned again. "You can either show me a picture of a style you like or let me make one up for you."

"And that's not using a wish?"

"Not at all."

"Ismail, you're a complete and total lifesaver." I bounced up and down on my toes. "I could kiss you!"

"Er, ah, um." All the suave went out of him. Ismail suddenly only had eyes for his feet.

"That's just another one of those modern expressions." I'd sure put my foot in my mouth. I hadn't been lying about wanting to kiss him, but for an old fashioned guy like Ismail, that was probably a million miles from appropriate in his perspective.

"Oh." He looked up a smidgen, but not at me. "Well, perhaps you ought to go and have breakfast."

My rumbling stomach didn't let me protest. I thanked Ismail again, just verbally. Then, I headed down to the dining hall. He vanished back into the lamp instead of following me. Once my plate was piled high with pancakes and enough butter and maple syrup to respect Vermont and clog the arteries of its population, I headed toward an empty table in the corner.

"Hey, Jean-bean!" Lynn Frampton had other ideas. She stepped in front of me. "We have some stuff to talk to you about."

"Huh?" The aroma of my poor, neglected pancakes made it difficult to think. And besides, with my recent spate of clumsiness, the last thing I wanted to do was stand there holding them.

"Just come sit here instead of whatever lonely crag you had in mind to have your chow." Lynn smirked and beckoned me to a booth. She gave me plenty of room to make a beeline, too. But of course, she was used to dealing with bear shifters around food. She was my cousin Bobby's mate, after all.

So I cut into my pancakes and shoveled food into my mouth for a few moments before I even realized Tony Gitano was there, sitting in the corner with Lynn blocking him in. I blinked and kept on eating. I didn't have a problem with him myself, no matter how bad things seemed between him and Blaine or how he and Ismail were like oil and water. He was almost a survivor, like me, Ismail, and Mr. Kazynski. But whatever he was weathering still had him in its teeth.

"Yeah, okay, so." Lynn rolled her eyes and sighed, twirling her spoon in the bowl of Captain Crunch in front of her. "Blaine threw his computer across the room last night. Kimiko had to salvage the data on it. She's a computer whiz, who knew. But anyway, that's beside the point. Before I go any further with this discussion, is Ismail around?"

"Do you want him to be?"

"Not really. I think you and Tony should hear this first." She glanced at my bag, over my head, out at the rest of the dining room, even under the table. "I have to do something to be absolutely sure, but the results won't be back until maybe eight tonight."

"Absolutely sure about what, Frampton?" Tony thrummed his fingers on the table so hard he jostled the milk in Lynn's bowl and the extra syrup on my plate.

"Sorry, getting ahead of myself again. Maybe it's better if I show you." Lynn reached under the table again, producing a manila envelope. She pushed it between Tony and me.

"You open it, Tony." I held out my sticky hands. "I'll end up making it look like something that belongs to Winnie the Pooh."

"Fine, whatever." Tony lifted the flap, then slid some papers out. They had the grainy, gray speckled look of copies run off on a machine that leaked too much toner. He shook his head at one, sliding it across to me. But his eyes went wide at the second one. "How the Hell did you get a picture of my mother, Frampton? And why is she dressed like an extra from Kings of New York?"

"I didn't. That's your great-grandma. She's dressed like that because she just got off a ferry from Ellis Island."

"Let me guess, the big dude with her is great-grandpa Pasquale."

"Yes. And he was..."

"A lion shifter. I know." Tony kept gazing at the picture, seemingly enthralled with the image. "And great-grandma was a leopard." He ran one hand down the lower half of his face.

"Yup. We think she was a Persian leopard shifter, actually."

"But wait. That'd mean she wasn't Italian."

"Maybe." Lynn held up one hand, opened it to reveal a plastic tube with a long cotton swab sticking out of it. "We don't know for sure. So that's why I have this."

"Is that some Jerry Springer baby daddy test thingamabob?" Tony leaned back, shrinking further into the corner than I thought possible. He clutched the photocopied picture to his chest. "I'm not taking that. If it comes out wrong and word gets out, things will go even worse for me."

"Hey, Tony." Lynn tilted her head. "Don't be a fraidy cat."

Tony told Lynn to go do something by herself that she probably preferred doing with her boyfriend. I set down my fork and knife, making a little 'x' on my plate. Then, I wiped my hands on the napkin and picked up the paper he'd pushed across to me.

"This here is a family tree, Tony." I scanned the names, dates, and connections. "It's public knowledge on a genealogy website, and it says your great-grandma emigrated to Italy before she married and got on the boat to America. Her previous origins are unknown. Lynn's DNA test won't make a lick of difference to this record, especially since she's not even supposed to have access to that kind of magical medical technology in her Freshman year. She won't let it leak, and since she's smart, she'll destroy it along with the results as soon as she's done."

I had to give Lynn credit. She didn't wither under both our glares, but she sure did squirm.

"Guys, I'm just doing what I have to. No one else in Tinfoil Hat has access to that lab, anyway." She actually wrung her hands. "I promise I'll have Maddie or Henry get rid of anything left of the sample. That Sprite still owes them each a favor, so it'll be like it never existed."

"Fine. I'll open my mouth but I ain't saying aah." Tony waited for Lynn to uncap the collection vial, then dropped his jaw. She swabbed his cheek. He closed his mouth and rubbed the side of his face. "Now, what is it you're trying to find out? It better be related to our big magical problem."

"It sort of is, because all this family tracking has to do with one of the targets." Lynn tightened the cap on the vial, then tucked it away in her bag. "I'm going to either confirm or rule out your relation to someone." She stared at me.

"Wait, what?" Tony blinked across the table at me, then looked down at the paper in his hand, then at his own reflection in the chrome napkin holder on the table. "No way am I related to the La Montagnes. I mean, I'm sure you're a great family and all, but you're French, and I'm full blood It—"

"Ismail." I couldn't stand all the weird assumptions and tangents anymore. They were like something out of an old comedy flick. "We're trying to find Ismail's descendants because I'm his lamp's third master. He'll be stuck in there forever if no one turns up."

Now that it was all laid out plainly like that, it seemed so simple and impossible. Even if Tony was a relation, he was a shifter, definitely not a Changeling. Only Magi or Psychics could be both. No way he could take over in any case. I shook my head, concerned about Ismail and the likelihood of his eternal service in the lamp. A guy like him shouldn't have to take orders like some kind of magical barista for the rest of time. And then Tony shockingly one-upped me on the plain speech front.

"And you finding out I'm his great-great-great something or other is going to help how?" Tony folded the paper and tucked it somewhere inside the trench coat he always wore. He looked away from us both. "Dammit, Lynn, I'm a shifter, not a Faerie."

"I know." She flipped her hair over one shoulder. "But you might have other relatives who are."

"Not from Great-grandpa Pasquale's side of the family, which is also my mom's." Tony shook his head. "Even if I'm your guy, that's a dead end."

"Hey, your mom might have had siblings, or maybe a brother or sister. Tell me about her." Lynn had utterly shattered the Tony Gitano code of asking too many questions without even realizing it.

"You let me up right now." Tony bristled. "You let me up or so help me, I'll tear you apart to get out of here. I don't give a whole bucket of rats that you're Bobby's girl, either."

Lynn slid out of the booth immediately, scrambling to get out of Tony's way. Something besides normal cat shifter stuff had me scrambling, too. Or maybe it was normal cat shifter stuff. Tony looked bigger than usual, his hair sticking out in all directions and his eyes gleaming bright green. My bear was up in a big way, enhancing my strength so I didn't know it. When I stood, I bumped the table. It tilted, then overturned like something out of a wrestling match.

Tony paid that calamity no mind, storming out the door without looking back. I caught a few mumbles about not trusting doctors or people who wanted to be them when they grew up.

"Well, that was unexpected."

"Lynn, never ask Tony about his family." I shook my head. "I mean, not ever. No one does."

"Well, I won't in the future. And you know, I think that didn't go so bad."

"Really? I can't think of a way it could have been worse."

"Hah." Her flat laugh made me look up from my attempt to right the table. "I can. Blaine could have been here, too."

I snorted, then gave up on the poor, wrecked booth. I hadn't just knocked the table over I'd demolished it. It'd torn from the base that welded it to the floor. My big, fat, unexplained klutz mojo had struck again, and I still had no idea how or why.

CHAPTER TWELVE

Ismail

My stomach fluttered as I waited for Jeannie to go about the rest of her day. I didn't listen in or watch this time, confused by my uncustomary nervousness. I'd check the hour, only to find the minutes had crawled into stretches that felt like hours. When I tried to talk to Neil, the mirror remained blank. I couldn't figure out why until I remembered that the charity event was partly his as well. The Senior Center'd had all its renovations done by his company, after all.

When the silver timepiece I kept in the lamp chimed six, Jeannie called to me. She'd decided to let me choose her attire. I stayed inside as I worked, weaving magic to create and embellish a garment to fit her from memory. I wasn't sure whether the new awkwardness between us had lingered and was afraid to find out. Once it was finished, I sent it out, along with a message that I would appear with her once she arrived at the venue.

The Senior Center couldn't accommodate a function with

dancing, so we'd be on the patio at the Capital Grille downtown. Fortunately, it was a warm April for New England. With that in mind, I went to work on my own attire while I waited. The task didn't make the hour seem to pass any faster. Of course, there wasn't much for me to do besides make some embellishments to my century-old style of dress.

The next time Jeannie called, I vanished myself out of the lamp to be at her side. I offered her my arm before taking in my surroundings, then gaped like a fish at the man-made lagoon before me.

"I figured you'd want to get a good look at Water Place Park before we've got a more crowded view of it." She squeezed my arm.

"Thank you." I didn't look at her yet because I wasn't done taking in this place she called a park.

It was almost perfectly round, with a canal leading out from one side like a spoke. Braziers lit with red fire dotted the canal, with five interspersed around the lagoon like the points of an invisible star. All around in a circle was a cobblestone path, with steps up and down in places and the occasional bench. I peered at a brightly lit area one-quarter of the way from us, realizing it was a passageway leading out to street level. The lights shone on murals, mosaics, and sculptures. Providence city planners had taken a tunnel and turned it into an art display, a brilliant stroke. But none of it held a candle to the dazzling woman on my arm.

I'd dressed her in gold, to match the lowlights in her hair. I hadn't noticed before that her blue eyes were flecked with the same color. Her smile was more precious than a strand of diamonds, her touch on my arm as warm as the light from the fires. I'd dared something with her dress, making it less a replica from Turkish days gone by and more what the modern Western media would expect. Perhaps that had been a mistake. Jeannie shivered a little, probably chilled by her arms and midriff left bare by its design.

When she leaned against me, no doubt for warmth, I tried not to gasp or pull away. I couldn't help but tense up.

"I'm sorry." She tilted her head as she gazed up at me. "It's warm for April, but still. I should know you're not like guys who grew up in these times, even if we're physically about the same age."

"Please don't apologize." I rolled my shoulders, attempting to relax. "These are the times I live in now. I should get used to change, too. It comes with the lamp's particular brand of time-travel."

"Is that a not-so-subtle hint that you don't think we'll find you a replacement in time?" She started walking, and I followed her lead.

"I don't think one exists."

"Pure Faeries exist."

"Good luck finding one who wants to risk being at the whim of mortals without the ability to trick them into asking questions and placing them in debt."

"Who knows, maybe there's one out there who actually likes mortals."

"Doubtful," I sighed. "Even if there were, the Monarchs wouldn't like losing any of their Pure. It'd be a major act of rebellion."

"I've heard stories about Pure Faeries rebelling before."

"Is this from during the, er, Reveal?" I'd censored myself even though she'd explicitly told me not to. "I didn't mean that. What I intended to ask was whether those stories are from your time in the Boston Internment."

"I'm glad you asked what you'd meant to." Her grin was wry, but there. "Yes and no. I've heard it more than once, on the barges, from a client. The most recent was a story Nox told me. But any retellings will have to wait. We're here."

I let Jeannie show the hostess her passes. We followed her out to the patio where the function had just begun. Small groups sat, six to each round table. Blaine and Kimiko were at ours, in costumes based on the Japanese feudal era. The Tanuki girl kept looking at me sideways. I dismissed it as curiosity since I'd barely left the lamp the entire time she'd had it.

The rest of our table seemed to be reserved for professors from the College. I scanned the room, looking for Nox the Kelpie, and spotted her by one of the fire exits in a Security t-shirt. A lanky blond man only slightly taller stood on the other side of the door, wearing similar attire. He nodded at Jeannie, who murmured that he was Josh, the Alpha mentioned at the Lounge the night before.

The table closest to us was occupied by the entire Redford family, dressed like pioneers, Neil, his wife, Fred, and a boy of about ten. There were also two others I didn't recognize, an older Troll man with another young enough to be his granddaughter. Squinting at their place cards told me these were the Tollands, ranked Admiral and Captain in the King's Navy. I'd heard of them, but we hadn't actually met.

Off to the left of what looked like a dance floor was a string quartet tuning up. Two elderly women sat with a cello and a bass. An old man with a viola turned out to be Saul Kazynski. The violinist was a young woman with jet-black hair in a braid on one side of her neck. She looked so much like Saul had in his younger days, I knew this had to be the granddaughter in the photo I'd seen on his mantle. I blinked when she plugged her instrument into an amplifier, intrigued.

"Forgive me for my ignorance, Jeannie, but I didn't know that violins are electric now."

"Yeah. It's more of an internet pop culture thing. Unless you've been keeping up by reading newspapers or watching TV, you wouldn't know about Irina Kazynski. She's graduating from the Boston Conservatory next month. Already has a huge YouTube following."

"So, this is truly an important event, then." I raised an

eyebrow. "A celebrity's donating her time to perform, Newport's first shifter family is sending a contingent even though they are allied with the Queen, and half the tenured faculty are here."

"Yeah, I told you." She patted my arm. "And I would have shown up in a cheap Halloween costume or a little black dress with a bunny ear headband if it weren't for you. Thanks again, Ismail." I glanced down at her, that smile of hers threatening to steal my breath again. Yeva never had that much of an effect on me.

"I'd do it again a million times over." Her blush was so deep a crimson that onlookers might have thought it made her look imperfect. To me, it only added to her charm.

Before I could say anything, a tired-looking woman with auburn hair and gray at the temples cleared her throat at the podium. There was no microphone, so she had to be an Air Magus. With those two clues, I knew this was Henrietta Thurston, Headmistress of Providence Paranormal College.

"Welcome, and thank you all for coming. It's been an interesting semester at the College, and eventful in an entirely different way than I could have expected."

Her voice rang out clear as a bell, but I could tell something in her energy was off. I'd heard the Headmistress worked hard, but that didn't account for the low level of magic around a woman of her age and skill level. I wondered whether some magic-leeching beastie or other hadn't been plaguing her as she slept. This distracted me so much I couldn't concentrate on the rest of her speech. At the end, she sat down at our table, across from Jeannie. A fellow about a decade older than her patted her arm from the seat reserved for a Professor Watkins. They grinned at each other.

Neil Redford took the podium next, talking about new improvements in the historic building which housed the Senior Center. Listening to him, I knew he'd found his passion in making things with his hands. The life Neil used to know, of wandering the frontier aimlessly, had never truly been him, a fact I remember shocking him with the night we met. And I remembered what he'd said to me in response, that I'd better find someone to love, or I'd turn into a whole heap of trouble.

When Neil introduced Jeannie, I understood exactly why attending this event was important enough for her not to go into hiding with Maddie, the Umbral Magus. If Neil's passion was building, Jeannie's entire reason for being was making sure the people in her care could get what they needed. She'd chosen the same path I had, but for all the right reasons. Instead of serving to run away from something, she'd made helping her life, to run toward people in need or at risk. That courageous concern lit the patio up more beautifully than the stars at her back.

At the end of her speech, Jeannie introduced the quartet, three of whom were seniors served by the Center. I could almost swear she could do magic because I felt almost like we took flight when she laced her arm through mine and led me to the dance floor. We waltzed among several other couples though I didn't bother much with looking at them.

"Jeannie, I think I want to tell you."

"Should we sit down?"

"No." I sighed as I spun her, watching as the spangles on her long skirt reflected light everywhere like a mirror ball. "It's better for me to be doing something while I speak about this, I think."

"Then go ahead. Say anything." She tilted her head again as she had on the way there. I took a deep breath and finally ran toward instead of away.

"After I came back from the Under, I told myself that my wife and children needed me in the lamp in case the unthinkable happened. And it did. The Young Turks rounded them up, but Yeva didn't summon me. They marched her into the deserts along with my son and daughter, and she didn't make a wish. I could have come out anyway, bent the rules like I've done for you. But I'd heard rumors. I couldn't bear to see them proved correct. I hadn't the stomach for it.

"And finally, Yeva wished to be rescued. But I couldn't bring myself to emerge beside her. I'd sensed some British Extrahumans on the other side of a dune. If they crested the ridge, they'd see everything. I left them a magical trail. After that, I dared to look. A massive rampaging dragon with blue and white scales spewed wind to rival a sandstorm from his mouth and rescued the victims."

"That was Wilfred Harcourt." The emotions in Jeannie's eyes mirrored mine: fear, sadness, a dash of guilt. She understood.

"I came to Yeva's aid too late to even see her fall. One of the guards stepped back, his scimitar red with blood. The children cowered back in fear as the man threatened them again. I knew what would come next, but I'd been a Magus as well as a Changeling before I tithed. My electrical magic was weak, but Yeva's death came with a surge of raw power. I burst free of the lamp, slinging a bolt of lightning at the murderer. The hair on the children's heads stood on end. The charcoal that was left of him clattered against the petrified lightning I'd made, then rolled down the dune."

"So it was Wilfred who brought your children and the others out of Turkey." She sighed. "No wonder you mourned him."

"Yes, and he took mastery of my lamp, as dragons do when they find something valuable. A Djinn serves three masters each time one takes a turn in a lamp, but because Yeva died after just one wish that went ungranted, she didn't count."

"What did he use his wishes on, if you don't mind my asking? And how did you end up at The Academy?" It was hard to think past the anguish, remembering it all caused, but Jeannie's questions helped me move along and change focus.

"Wilfred returned to Turkey, rescuing any Extrahumans he could find. He exchanged their freedom for heirlooms, but it didn't lower my opinion of him. A cowardly Djinn can't exactly judge a profiteering dragon. He did the same during the Second World War. I helped when I could without using a wish, granting three over a span of decades. After that, he could have passed me to anyone. Instead, he left me in a peace I sorely desired back in those days. And then, he married Hertha. She couldn't tolerate an Unseelie Djinn under her roof, so he donated my lamp to The Academy for study. When a certain Tanuki girl stole it and brought me back to Wilfred's home, I hoped to see him again, but coincidence had other ideas. I was left to pay my respects instead."

"Well, it's a good thing I haven't made any official wishes yet, then." She gazed up at me. "I can't even imagine being stuck in there forever, especially after you've been through all that. A profiteering dragon and a cowardly Djinn turned out to be heroes. You deserve your freedom. Besides," she grinned, "I'm not sure I want you designing gorgeous outfits for random women for the rest of time."

I didn't want to look away from her, but a tug at my sleeve meant I had to turn my head to see who dared vie for my attention. And I found myself frowning down at Kimiko Ichiro.

"Ismail, can I cut in? I have to talk to you."

"You see me out here, trying to actually live a little as you always said I should, and decide to interrupt it?" I softened the frown. Kimiko was wily but ultimately meant well. "Perhaps it can wait?"

Movement from behind her caught my eye. Blaine fidgeted at the edge of the parquet dance floor, glancing back and forth between Headmistress Thurston and the Professor with her, a man named Watkins. I couldn't see magic energy around him, so he had to be Psychic. But he looked almost as worse for wear as the Headmistress.

"It can't." Kimiko's eyes widened, and her mouth dropped open as she looked at Jeannie and me, then out at the lagoon the patio overlooked. "It's your Luck. Not you, your lamp's. It's turning the wrong way. That's why Jeannie keeps having accidents, and everything you try to do is harder. It's gone bad in a big—"

Before Kimiko could finish what she was saying, a shower of cold, brackish water rained down on us. Jeannie's foot slipped in it, sending us both to the ground in a heap.

A monstrous, hulking, amalgamated thing had risen out of the pool at the center of Water Place Park, and no one at that illustrious gathering seemed to have the slightest idea what to do about it.

CHAPTER THIRTEEN

Jeannie

I didn't know what that thing was besides ugly and enormous. It defied all Extrahuman or magical creature classification in my experience or education. Neil Redford stood up to it but got sent flying through the glass between the patio and the restaurant's main dining room for his trouble. If it could land a blow on a Redcap that old, it'd be able to smack me for sure.

I shifted anyway. The outfit Ismail had made me didn't tear into a million little pieces, just fell away like magic because that's what it was. I let out a roar, unleashing the universal sign for "angry bear." Josh Dennison had the same idea, howling up at the sky in what could only be a rallying cry. I never thought I'd hear hooves on parquet flooring, but Nox galloped beside us, her Water magic frothing up under her feet and flying from her mane in a shield against whatever that attacking creature was.

My ears twitched, and I wondered why both the Kazynskis were still playing. They'd gone from waltzes to The Devil Went

Down to Georgia. A sudden impulse to kick whatever passed for the mysterious creature's butt invaded my heart and mind like the aliens in The Day The Earth Stood Still.

"Luck tuuuuuuuurn!" Kimiko sounded like she was auditioning for a stage production of *Inu Yasha* and looked like she was doing the Macarena. Unfortunately, the whole effect and whatever Luck energy manipulation she'd intended failed when a ball of goo knocked her back. She floundered on the floor in her now-sodden costume. A heavy goblet rolled off the table above her and conked her on the noggin, and Kimiko went down for the count.

A rush of air whooshed behind me, and an angry reptilian cry rose in response to the Tanuki getting served. Blaine Harcourt's big red dragon body stood on the steps between the attacker and us. He opened his mouth and promptly got a throat full of slime. His head and neck swayed as his scales paled from red to his usual skin tone, then, he shrank back to his human form right there in the creature's path. I wondered how we were going to beat this thing if it had magic gunk that could knock us out of our shifted forms.

"The goo's enchanted!" I heard Maddie's voice coming from somewhere even though I couldn't see her.

I watched Captain Gemma Tolland try to run for the steps leading down to the middle of Water Place Park. She dropped her glamour completely, revealing wilder hair and eyes than usual, plus a set of delicate, pearly tusks protruding from her lower lip. I'd never seen a Troll get angry before. Spikes sprouted across her back and down her arms, growing along with her rage. But just before she could go full-out Troll Berserker, Admiral Tolland sent a beam of silver light straight at her. It lassoed her waist, and he dragged her back with him into the restaurant and out of the battle. It made sense. Admiral Tolland had a reputation for not getting involved in mortal affairs unless he got paid.

Without Gemma as a target of opportunity, the thing went straight for Fred's little brother.

"Not my baby!" Mrs. Redford was a Psychic Medium and thank goodness she'd brought her ghosts. "Get em' guys!"

When ghosts attacked, no one could see them unless they were Mediums or had some sort of Psychic device. I knew they were fighting because of the glasses and cups hurtling through the air, thrown by invisible hands. Even when they moved on to chucking chairs and tossing tables, the thing seemed unharmed. It just absorbed the furniture. But the thing turned away and left the Redford kid alone. That gave Josh Dennison and the rest of Tinfoil Hat's shifters exactly the opening they needed.

Josh darted forward, joined by a three-legged wolf bounding up from the bottom of the steps. That'd be his sister, Beth. A sleek, furry form splashed in the water, too, flanking the creature directly inside the lagoon. They dipped and weaved, distracting the thing long enough to protect Blaine and the Redfords until Fred got them out of the way. They all vanished into a patch of shadow in one corner of the patio, but Fred came back out almost immediately.

"It's some kind of golem!" Fred shouted in our general direction and past us. Golems took a concerted effort of mortal magic, Psychic energy, and Faerie powers. For all I knew, there could be an army of Extrahumans powering the thing. I remembered Ismail behind me. I could use a wish if only I knew what would get rid of the thing attacking us. Maybe I needed to think of something besides banishing it.

"On it, sonny boy!" Neil Redford picked bits of The Capital Grille's plate-glass window out of his sharp, pointy teeth and shook more off his now-massive and gray-skinned frame. He'd eaten the window he'd crashed into and gone full Redcap, dropping his glamour to call extra power from the Under. Fred's dad leaped and bounded across to where Professor Watkins and Headmistress Thurston lay prone on the floor. He reached for

Watkins as Ismail extended his arm toward the Headmistress. At least the unconscious faculty members wouldn't get caught in the crossfire.

"No more ironic Unseelie heroics, Neil." Professor Watkins sat up, and I grunted in shock. His eyes were glassy and his limbs oddly limp, like he was either boneless or not moving under his own power. His voice was all wrong, too, like someone else was using his mouth to speak. I remembered Professor Brodsky, a Psychic Summoner victimized by Mind magic, and wondered if this was something similar.

Neil scratched his head, shrugging at the floppy professor as though he couldn't figure out what kind of threat he posed. That was when the thing from the lagoon slapped one of its long limbs across his face, knocking him out cold. Ismail jumped back and out of the way just in time. A renewed surge of music met my ears as the string quartet played faster. Something had amplified them, but I wasn't sure what. Their audio equipment looked fried. But Saul Kazynski had Psychic powers to affect emotions. That had to be it.

The strike against Neil was a sucker-punch, and I knew it. I looked for the other attack, wondering where the next blow would fall. But why hadn't the creature killed any of Tinfoil Hat, or Neil Redford, for that matter? Why would it pull its punches? And then I remembered that coincidence would slap any magic back on the caster. They'd all been attacked before, or in Neil's case, places he'd put his heart, soul, and magic into building. This had to be the work of the Extramagus.

I was too late to block it when the creature flung one of the tables it had absorbed at the string quartet. I watched Irina Kazynski turn her instrument toward the incoming barrage, amazed that her music changed its course. It would have crushed her grandpa if she hadn't. As it was, it slammed into his leg. I heard a wet snap, and he went down with a cry.

I snarled at Ismail, who crouched beside Headmistress

Thurston. Wishes needed intent and words, but if I shifted, Josh and half his pack would be left to fight all by themselves. I used a claw to gouge two words in the slate of the patio, nonspecific and possibly a waste of a wish, but it worked. Ismail nodded, and a shield of crackling energy went up around the string quartet. Amazingly, Saul Kazynski and the rest kept on playing.

"Give me the lamp and the bear shifter and I'll let the rest of you escape with your lives." The voice coming from Professor Watkins' mouth was even more wrong than before, like he wasn't in his body anymore.

Josh growled, Nox snorted, and Beth barked, echoed by one which sounded like a seal from the lagoon. That had to be Ren Ichiro, Kimiko's Selkie brother. I refused to be left out or let the kids in Tinfoil Hat fight this battle for me, so I roared again and led the charge.

If the Extramagus wanted me, they'd have to deal with my fangs and claws first!

Ismail

I watched Jeannie leap from the top of the steps outside the patio, closing the gap between her and the creature. I couldn't let her grapple it. I knew what would happen. A golem like this had devoured an Allied platoon on the European Front in the Second World War before Wilfred and I stopped it. I'd held back this time because I told myself one of the high-status, wealthy guests would handle it, but they'd all either fled or fallen, and I had let a group of youngsters fight a battle I should have been at the front of. Two were unconscious, and the golem had injured one of my few remaining friends. Now it had hurt Jeannie. I couldn't let that happen. I wouldn't run away this time, even though I didn't have an Air dragon backing me up.

"Stop playing and fight!" I threw a punch toward the creature to direct my magic. I wasn't breaking any rules of the lamp to do it, either. This was the magic I'd grown up with—lightning. It struck, arcing over and around the golem in a blue and yellow honeycomb of lines and spaces.

Its surface rippled, the electricity jolting it. The pit of my stomach dropped when I remembered the Selkie in the water with it, but it was too late to take it back. It'd be too late for much of anything soon. If the golem devoured me with its acidic slime, I'd reform back in the lamp to grant Jeannie's last two wishes. After that, I'd die. I stood, holding lightning in my hands so at least I'd go down fighting, and maybe even take it with me. And then I heard Jeannie.

"I wish for no one in this entire state to suffer a golem's harm from this moment forward!"

"I call on the Under to help me grant this wish!" I took a deep breath, knowing her attempted wish would be useless. Only one of the Monarchs could make a ban that big and include a construct so powerful.

"My debt to you is paid, Marquess Ismail." The Goblin King stood between me and the golem. He snapped his fingers and the creature stopped, settling itself back in the lagoon. Whoever was controlling it mustn't know what to do with it now.

"Debt?" I blinked at his back, noting that he still wore the same dusty brown hunting boots, gray riding pants, and purple leather vest over a frilly shirt as he'd done a hundred years ago. "I had no idea you owed me anything but a place in your Court."

"Why, yes." He smirked, tapping the leg of his boot with a riding crop. "Your mistress saved my favorite bard's life, although you couldn't have known that at the time. That was the reason I gave him my favor, and the reason I can enable you to grant this shifter's wish tonight."

"Thank you, Your Majesty." I bowed to him as I'd done in the Under after I'd tithed.

"I must warn you, Marquess. You'll get no more direct help from me for the rest of the evening." He flicked his long black hair over one shoulder. "I like this new you, Ismail. Fare thee well, and let your heart lead you." With another snap of his fingers, he vanished much more neatly than I'd ever been able to do.

"Well, that was unexpected." Maddie emerged from the shadowy corner, holding one end of a big duffel bag. A golden-skinned man in surf shorts held the other. He ran a hand through his slightly singed brown hair and resembled Kimiko so closely that I knew my magic hadn't seriously injured the Selkie. They dropped articles of clothing near the other shifters so they'd have something to wear as they changed back. I saw what looked like a Sprite dashing toward the hole in the plate-glass window, then rubbed my eyes and looked again.

"That wasn't really a Sprite I just saw?" I looked around for an answer. Jeannie headed over, wearing a pink sundress. I put my arm around her, but before either of us could say anything, someone else did. We walked together toward the string quartet.

"Good old Ismail, questioning everything no matter what's happened." Saul's strained voice came from behind the Lightning shield I hadn't dropped yet. I took it down and headed over to him.

"It's too late for me to heal this, old friend." I placed my hand on his leg.

"I'll call an ambulance. This has pockets!" Jeannie grinned and pulled a phone out of the dress. Clearly, the bag was part of some preparation on the part of the Tinfoil Hat pack.

"Thank you." The lines on Saul's face lost some of their sharpness. "I know you can't reverse it after this much time." He was talking about the Gnomish magic that came with my lamp. One had lived in it before the Monarchs had split, so with a wish, I could have reversed the injury during the first five seconds after it took place. "But what will you do about the golem?"

"I'm not sure." The thing was still in the middle of Water Place Park. Jeannie sat with Saul and the other two elderly musicians. Saul's granddaughter was nowhere to be seen.

"Well, we have to do something about it." Blaine Harcourt hobbled over, wearing a towel and leaning on Kimiko. "It's draining Professor Watkins and the Headmistress every minute it stays there. Whoever sent it must have done a major group casting before with their help because they're tapped into it. If we don't tear that thing down fast, the two of them will die."

"Does anyone happen to have an Air dragon they can call?" I stood and began pacing the exact dimensions of my lamp out of habit. "Because that was how we did it last time. It's the only way without a Null Magus."

"Well, no. We don't have either of those." Blaine shook his head, eyelids drooping. "Let me guess: my fiery halitosis won't do it."

"You're in no condition to shift right now anyway." Kimiko squeezed his hand. "It needs extreme cold, not an inferno."

"Perhaps I can be of service." The vaguely familiar voice came from behind me.

Blaine jerked his head up, straining to try to stand up straight or otherwise look presentable. I recognized who'd just spoken.

"You're the librarian." I turned to look at the older man.

"Yes. Taki Waban is my name, and I am an ice dragon. Will that do?" His smile set his black eyes twinkling.

"Even better than Air." I chuckled. "Wilfred had to use most of his strength to cool the golem enough for me to shatter it. With ice breath, it should go much quicker."

He walked down the steps to the area in front of the lagoon. In dragon form, Taki Waban was black with a silvery sheen of frost on his scales. He was also bigger than Blaine, but serpentine and able to fit in tighter quarters as a result. He breathed on the golem, freezing it in seconds. I went as far as the second step on the stone staircase, then focused my magic again. My Lightning blast sent bits of it hurtling into the air and then back down to splatter into the water like an extremely localized rainstorm.

Right there, amidst all that confusion, Jeannie stood on the top step, placed her hands on my shoulders, and kissed me. I embraced her, running my hands up her back and then through her hair. She left me so breathless, I almost tumbled down the stairs. We grinned, not caring when some of the strange rain missed the water and fell on us and the patio, too.

"Whahappen?" Headmistress Thurston stirred, reaching out with her hands as though trying to grasp something. She bumped one foot into Neil Redford, who lay there groaning and clutching his head.

Professor Watkins didn't move. Jeannie returned to my side. We sat and watched his chest barely rise and fall. I put my arm around her again. Kimiko turned the Luck on my lamp back in the right direction. The Redfords went home together. All the shifters got dressed. Maddie called back her shadows. We agreed to stay with the wounded.

When the ambulances got there, the EMEs did their triage. They rushed away with Saul Kazynski and the Headmistress but took their time with Professor Watkins.

"Do you know what that means?" I nodded at the response of the medical people.

"No, but there's someone we can ask." Jeannie got up and held a hand down to me. "Come on, Ismail. We're supposed to meet Lynn about your descendants. It's a pretty good walk, so we should start now."

CHAPTER FOURTEEN

Jeannie

We got all the way up to Hope Street before he said anything, but Ismail let me hold his hand the entire way.

"You used one of your wishes to protect the entire state, Jeannie." He didn't stop walking or even turn his head to look at me. "Why is that?"

"Because I'm a bear. I might have grown up in Boston, but this is the place I picked for myself." I shrugged. "So I won't just leave things so some nutcase Extramagus can attack people with something like that whenever they want."

"Did you know that I can see records of all the wishes made with my lamp?" We walked along in silence for almost a block because I was ashamed to give him the answer.

"No. Didn't have any idea." I forced a stiff chuckle. "Can you believe they're letting me graduate in a couple of weeks?"

"I doubt anything so complicated as the function of ancient Faerie artifacts was a required subject matter for your major."

"Still, I feel downright ignorant after dealing with all this." I sighed. "Like maybe I'm not ready."

"Are we ever ready, though?" This time, he did look at me. "I graduated from college, tithed and spent my time in the Under. And I thought I was ready for everything. But I wasn't. I still might not be."

We turned the corner and walked along the long side of the lot Josh Dennison's big giant historic house was situated on. I noticed the wrought-iron fencing had all been torn down. It sat in a pile near where Ismail stepped in front of me, stopping so we could finish this conversation before meeting the others.

"Okay, so what's your point about readiness, then?" I put my hands on my hips. After doing all that work to bring Ismail out of his figurative and literal shell, I felt like I wanted to take a turn in one myself.

"The point is, whether you feel ready or not, you can't stop." He held his hands out in front of him, palms up at waist height. "You can't run away, either, because the fear's inside. It'll just follow you wherever you go. So when you say you're not ready, I say it doesn't matter. You don't have to be ready, you only have to keep moving forward. You helped me learn that, Jeannie La Montagne. And that's only one of the things I love about you."

I dropped my hands off my hips, then reached out to take both of his. As our fingertips touched, a flare of light blinded me. All I could see was a slim silhouette of someone with what looked like a cane, but I was wrong about that last bit.

"Lovely speech. Excellent last words." I'd never heard that voice before but I knew right away it was male. "I've finally gotten one over on you meddling kids, and I didn't even have to use a spell to do it."

The part of the figure I'd mistaken for a cane turned out to be one of the iron spikes. I realized that when the bloody end of it protruded from Ismail's chest. I stared at the figure again, but it vanished with the light. Spots and shapes danced in front of my eyes, and my stomach fell like an elevator with a severed cable. I sank to the ground holding Ismail and screaming.

"I wish this never happened!" My tears wet Ismail's face along with the blood at the corner of his mouth.

"Your wish, my command." He smiled and closed his eyes. I couldn't look away. The bloody tinge around his teeth turned pink, then vanished. I heard a metallic clang and turned my head to see the fence post drop back on top of the pile with the rest. When I looked back, every trace of the fatal wound was gone. The only way I knew it hadn't just been my imagination was the fact that we were both on the sidewalk instead of standing.

"Oh, no." I put my hands on my cheeks, head rushing with the gravity of my mistake. "Oh, now I've done it."

"Done what?"

"Trapped you in that lamp forever. And after we've gone and fallen in love." I sniffled. Couldn't help it. The Extramagus had probably wanted me to watch Ismail die, but watching him lose his freedom forever because of me was almost as bad.

"We still have one hour before I'm trapped forever." Ismail got up and dusted himself off. It was his turn to give me a hand up, like I'd done for him back at Water Place Park. "It's not over yet. Let's see what your friend has for us."

"Which friend?" Josh Dennison looked from me to Ismail and back again. "You've got about ten of them up there at the house. And what was that light? Wait, never mind. Tell me up there because they'll all want to know, and it's no fun repeating a story that many times."

We followed him to the basement. Everyone was there. Ismail stopped on the threshold. I realized that not even the Ball had been this crowded. At least there, we'd been under an open sky. Here, every seat was taken, and every surface in use somehow, from drinks on the bar to a study station set up on a board atop the billiards table.

"You okay?"

"I used Gnomish powers from my lamp to time reverse an iron bar through my gut, and you ask if I'm okay walking into a crowded room." Ismail's chuckle was tiny and soft, but still there.

"I just wanted to be sure you could handle it."

"Of course. I'm with you."

Josh cleared his throat three times before the room quieted down enough for Ismail and me to tell them all what had happened on the sidewalk just over the Dennison property line. When we finished, I counted to three before the room erupted in outrage.

"—actually did that to a Djinn!"

"—timey-wimey mojo or he'd be—"

"Who even uses iron bars anymore, I mean seriously..."

"—drop flaming fewmets on his head!"

"—sure it's a dude now, thank Lady Luck."

"—should check him for iron fragments anyway—"

"Leaping Luna!"

"—liverwurst sandwich down his throat and pitch him head-first into the Under!"

"And after the Goblin King showed up..."

"—just glad he's alive."

It all stopped when a sound like a gunshot rang out through the room. Everyone turned to look. Tony Gitano stood holding a broken pool cue and quivering with anger. I wondered how breaking a stick could have sounded remotely like a shotgun. Before I could figure it out, he spat two words.

"Shut. Up." The thinner end of the cue dropped out of Tony's right hand. He hefted the larger in his left, flipping it so he held the jagged end in his palm. "You all are forgetting something." He pointed the cue at me. "Miss Perfect here just sent her boyfriend up Shit Creek without a paddle and you're all acting like a typical bunch of spooked Millenials. Cut. It. Out!" He hit a barstool, a chair, and the pool table with each word.

"So, what do you think we should do then, Tony?" Even leaning against the bar, Josh's entire stance dripped authority.

"Actually solve some problems for once. Oh, and maybe quit freaking out and slacking off."

"Hey!" Lynn stared daggers and Tony sure as Hell felt it.

"I wasn't talking about you, Frampton." Tony waved his free hand in her general direction. "I may not like your nosy methods, but you're the only one besides me who isn't too scared or lazy to do something constructive."

"Shut up, Puss-In-Converse!" The smoke around Blaine's head looked like Mount St. Helen's. "You have no right to tell me how to act. You haven't lost anyone!"

"Exactly. My. Point." He slapped the pool cue against his hand this time. "And none of you have any idea what I've been doing."

"You keep mentioning a point, Tony, so get to it." Josh thrummed his fingertips on the top of the bar. I saw that an empty beer bottle was in easy reach of his free hand.

"You all gotta do more than what you have been." He turned his back on Josh, "Here's the list of casualties so far, in case you haven't been keeping track. Two vampires, killed by the Grim. Professor Brodsky's sanity. Wilfred Harcourt, who should have been immortal. Kazynski's hip. Ismail's freedom. Professor Watkins."

"Wait, what?" Lynn blinked back tears. My own eyes stung, too.

"No!" Nox stood up. "That can't be true."

"I've been monitoring CB all night because I'm not fooling around here." Tony tapped the Bluetooth earpiece he always wore. "He's in a vegetative state. Brodsky's trial is this fall. If we can get more dirt on the Extramagus than that he's got cajones instead of teats, that's evidence. We could undo a little of the damage, at least, and prevent that slippery twit from killing anyone else."

"Granted." Josh nodded at Tony. "We'll step things up. Exams are almost over, and we're all free this summer. But what's this about Ismail's freedom? I thought our brainiac was on that."

"There isn't anyone." Lynn sighed, resting her head in her hands. "Ismail's only living relative is a shifter. Unless someone has a pure Faerie in their pocket, the Extramagus won on that front."

"Wait a minute." Henry smiled, which was like someone jumping out of a box at the Factory of Terror haunted house up in Fall River. Vampires got their blood from hospitals and Henry Baxter took pains to be sure he was well-fed at all times, but his fangs were still pretty unsettling. What he said next made me think he looked like an angel. "I actually have one of those."

"You don't mean Gee Nome?" Ren Ichiro shook his head. "There's no way Gee'd agree to live in a lamp forever. They like sneaking around too much."

"And it would definitely be forever, too, if a pure Faerie took my place." Ismail sighed. "They don't technically have relatives, so there's no way out unless both Monarchs agree to release them."

"No, not Gee. Ren's right, and besides, I like having that Gnome around." Henry chuckled. Maddie rushed to his side and hugged him.

"Oh, Henry, it's the perfect idea!" She bounced up and down on the balls of her feet, her wide, bright smile gleaming out from the dusky skin of her face. Maddie May was easily the happiest looking Goth girl I'd ever seen.

"Hoo, boy." Olivia's excitement got swallowed by her yawn. " The Spite. I mean, the ex-Spite. I mean the Sprite, they're a Sprite now, right? The one hiding from the Queen?"

"Yup." Henry grinned this time, more aware now of the effect his smile had on the rest of the room. "I'll call them. Even gave them a name so we wouldn't have to say 'hey, you.' Hey, Sparky," he called, "come out and have a chat with me."

A spindly-limbed creature crawled out from under the billiards table. They had tawny skin and wore what looked like one of Josh's old PPC Security t-shirts, altered to fit. Two holes in the back let their wings out, but everyone could see the Sprite couldn't exactly fly anymore. The poor thing had only ragged tatters left where the delicate membranes of nearly transparent skin should have been. The Sprite held an ornately carved wooden box under one arm.

"I'm here, Henry Baxter." They nodded at the vampire. "Are you using the last of the favors I owe you?"

"Yes and no, Sparky." It hurt my heart a little that Henry had given the poor creature a nickname. That pain eased when I saw them give him a toothy grin.

"I see. This Djinn needs a replacement." It kept its distance from Ismail, which made sense considering Sprites were Seelie creatures. But, if they used to be a Spite, one of the Queen's vicious hunting hounds, no wonder they tolerated the King's subjects. "And I need a home, someplace where even the Queen can't harm me."

"Yeah, but I think that's too tall an order for what you owe me." Henry shrugged. "Still, it's up to you. Are you willing to give up your freedom like that, Sparky?"

"Yes, but on one condition." They looked at Maddie when they spoke, not at Henry. "You hide the lamp in Billy Taylor Park, where the Kelpie freed me."

"Wait, what?" Maddie tilted her head, bouncing her curls. "But it's a public place."

"All the same," the Sprite replied, "those are my terms to make this agreement."

"That's so risky, though." Lynn shook her head. "Anyone who bumps into the lamp will know it's there and pick it up."

"No, I agree with Sparky." Tony tilted his head. "You have to put the lamp in the park."

"Why in Tiamat's name would *you* be cool with something like that, cat-man?"

"Because Sprites can see patterns in coincidence. If Sparky

wants to be there, they have a reason." Tony cleared his throat, then mumbled, "and I owe them a favor."

"That would repay both debts, leaving me free to occupy the lamp without conflict of interest." Sparky's nod might have been sage if they hadn't looked like a hairless kid. "I will take Duke Ismail's place."

"Thank you." Ismail chuckled. "But I'm a Marquess, not a Duke."

"Nope." Nox squinted at Ismail. "Sparky's right. You must have seriously impressed the King back there at Water Place. You leveled up. Gratz!"

"Um, can we get this done, please?" I pointed at the clock above the bar. "We only have a few minutes left."

I took the lamp out of my bag, placing it on the billiards table and opening the top. Ismail and Sparky held it between them, each reciting in two different languages I couldn't understand. Purple smoke flowed out of the lamp toward Ismail, while yellow motes of light swirled around Sparky's side, entering through the lid I'd opened. Something I can only describe as a reverse flash ended with Sparky hovering above the lamp. They waved at us and vanished inside.

The smoke around Ismail had coalesced into shackles on his wrists and ankles, joined by lengths of chain. When Sparky vanished, the magical bonds flew into a billion dark purple pieces, then dissipated. Ismail was free.

CHAPTER FIFTEEN

Ismail

I stood there grinning at Jeannie as I rubbed my wrists. Then, I leaned down and kissed her full on the mouth, more deeply and passionately than the quick one back at Water Place Park. The room filled with cheers and whistles I was only vaguely aware of. When I pulled away, she flung her arms around my neck as though she'd never let go.

"What was that for?"

"I just wanted to see what it was like kissing you now that I'm a free Djinn."

"Did you like it?" She smiled.

"I can't even begin to describe how much."

"Enough to want to do it again?"

I gave her an encore which went longer than the performance it followed. I lost track of time, possibly even the rest of the world. It differed completely from forgetting the months or seasons in the lamp. Somehow the fact I knew it would be fleeting made it feel more eternal.

"Um, I don't want to break up the schmooping, so sorry." It was a woman's voice. "But we kind of promised to do something."

I felt a tug on my sleeve. Jeannie and I broke it off to see Maddie staring at my hand. I hadn't even realized I'd still been holding the lamp.

"Oops."

The Umbral Magus shrugged and gave me a half-smile, then held out her hands. I dropped my old home into them. She headed toward the door with Tony and Henry.

"You want me to go, too?" Nox strode toward the door. Josh stopped her.

"Don't. Henry's got enough on his plate, having to change three memories. Why add to it?"

"Good point." She went back to the bar and what looked like a root beer float but smelled like alcohol.

"Did you want a Jaeger and root beer float?" Jeannie led me over to the bar. "I could go for one myself right about now."

"Hmm. I'm intrigued, but I might be too much of a light-weight for that."

"I'll get you some wine, then." Jeannie went back behind the bar and poured.

With Tony gone, the rest of the room seemed to relax. I understood now that he wasn't a spy or untrustworthy. The cat shifter just didn't want everyone knowing everything about him. Perhaps he'd even gotten that trait from me. I'd have to keep as much of an eye on him as he'd allow. I was his thrice-great grandfather, after all. And from what I'd heard and seen so far, he trusted his family less than his packmates. He might need my help before long.

"Okay, so we have some more information now." Josh got his phone out and woke it up. "Let's tell LORA the Extramagus is male for sure." He kept on tapping, swiped, then put the phone back in his pocket. "Tony was right about something. We've been dropping the ball too many times, so let's put our heads together and keep it in the air. Any theories?"

"I have one." I twirled the wineglass between my fingers, watching the light play across the golden liquid inside.

"Shoot." Josh leaned against the billiard table.

"It's rare, but it does happen that Psychics and Magi have other powers." I took a deep breath, knowing how controversial my idea might be. "I think he might also be a Changeling."

"But he can't be." Josh shook his head. I hadn't expected an Alpha open-minded enough to befriend a flightless Sprite to protest. But it turned out he had an excellent reason. "All the evidence points to him being Henry's age or older. And he was born in the 1970s. How could a Changeling go that long being untithed?"

"Yeah. I'm a wreck over having to tithe this summer." Fred's forehead crinkled as he frowned. "It sucks. I hoped I'd at least make it through Junior year. Guess that's what I get for taking a year off to work for Dad."

"You're not a Magus—"

"You're not a Psychic—"

Lynn let out a belly laugh while Blaine chuckled at their conversational collision. I waited, hoping one of the so-called brains in the pack figured it out. Lynn spoke first, still slapping her knee.

"If the Extramagus has all those mortal powers, he'd be able to hold off using his Faerie magic just about all the time. Using that is what makes Changelings need to tithe young. He could still be Henry's age."

"Yeah, you're right." Fred sighed. "Guy has all that power, and he uses it for homicide. Just think of all the things he could be building."

"Hmm." Blaine scratched his chin. "Dragons waste their energy like that, too. But on paranoia."

"Hey, you resemble that remark." Kimiko punched him in the arm.

"Yeah, but everyone knows I'm a stereotype-defying dragon." He winked at her. "What I mean to say is, maybe we should make guesses about this guy more like he's a dragon than a Magus. I mean, he's definitely paranoid, uses other people or creatures to do his dirty work, keeps all his awesomesauce for his own waffles. Maybe that stuff will help us predict what he'll do next instead of just to whom."

I was beginning to get the idea that half of the group had paired off. That might be another source of the tension I'd sensed. I wondered why everyone was looking at Fred. Apparently, so did he.

"What are you all staring at?" His surly expression changed to one of alarm. "My glamour's not down again, is it?"

"Nope." Nox kicked back the dregs of her alcoholic float. "They think you're next."

"Wait, what? Why?" His eyes got almost as big as his mouth. It made sense to me once they mentioned it.

"Your father helped me, then went after the golem tonight," I answered because no one else had all the information, and it was my theory, anyway. "So did you. Needing to hold off tithing makes you vulnerable. And if the Extramagus is a Changeling, he's planning to go Seelie. You're a Duke's son. Neil's the King's man. Which way are you going?"

"GK, all the way." Fred waved one index finger in the air like a half-hearted cheer. His stomach rumbled in counterpoint.

"There you are, then." I raised my glass to him. "May you have more success against him than I did."

Glasses all around the room clinked. Fred stomped to the fridge, got out a can of beer, and bit it to guzzle down the contents.

"But who else is next?" Jeannie scratched her head. "Back in the lounge, you said he always targets pairs."

"That's curious." I sipped my wine, trying to keep a grin off my face. "Tell that to this Lora person you've got helping you and see what she comes up with."

"Silly, Djinn!" Kimiko smirked. "You know all about LORA."

"That I do." I winked. "Tell your program that the Extramagus might be embittered. Perhaps he's lost a mate or never found one. He's picking his victims by coincidence patterns, right?"

"Yeah, that's what we think." Blaine raised an eyebrow and blew a smoke ring.

"He's looking for destined lovers, then."

"How do you figure?" Fred crushed his now empty beer can and tossed it into the blue bin.

"Lynn and Bobby. Henry and Maddie. Josh and Nox. Kimiko and Blaine. And now me and Jeannie." I glanced at Olivia. She was sleeping in an easy chair. Fred hadn't looked at her once.

"Cool theory, bro." Fred laughed. "But you're wrong. My head's in school and work every hour I'm not sleeping or with my family. I don't have time for girls."

"As you say." I just smiled at him. Fred Redford had no idea what he was in for as far as romance went. Unsurprising, considering Neil had waited so long to find a bride. The apple didn't fall far from the tree in the Redford line. Fortunately, the conversation moved along to other ideas, with background given to Jeannie and me as they went. The group of them who'd been targeted by the Extramagus before me had some interesting stories to tell.

I might have found myself more at ease with this group than I'd felt in a century, but I wasn't about to discuss how I'd felt about love before getting to know Jeannie. That was for her ears only. I wanted another hundred years to tell my feelings to her. Looking in her eyes, I knew she shared my wish.

ROUNDTABLE REDCAP

The series continues with *Roundtable Redcap* available now at Amazon and Kindle Unlimited.

Claim your copy today!

CONNECT WITH THE AUTHOR

Find D.R. Perry Online

Website: https://drperryauthor.com/

Author Central: http://www.amazon.com/-/e/B00O6851HO

Facebook: https://www.facebook.com/drpperry/

Mailing List: https://app.mailerlite.com/webforms/
landing/p9i8u6

Twitter: https://twitter.com/DRPerry22

OTHER LMBPN PUBLISHING BOOKS

To be notified of new releases and special promotions from LMBPN publishing, please join our email list:

http://lmbpn.com/email/

For a complete list of books published by LMBPN please visit the following pages:

https://lmbpn.com/books-by-lmbpn-publishing/